# BEAGLES LOVE CUPCAKE CRIMES

A SMALL TOWN CULINARY COZY MYSTERY

BEAGLE DINER COZY MYSTERIES

C. A. PHIPPS

*For my mum.*
*I'll always miss you.*
*Love you to the moon and back.*
*xoxoxo*

# BEAGLES LOVE CUPCAKE CRIMES

**Is this *Murder, She Baked?***

Lyra St. Claire is a celebrity chef and cooking is all she's ever wanted to do. Being plucked from school and thrown into the limelight was not the plan, and when everything goes wrong, she yearns for her hometown and a simpler life.

But before she can make any changes, she must find the murderer. Could it be the same person who wants to ruin her career?

If you love cooking wrapped around a mystery, then this is the series for you!

*You'll find a great recipe at the end of the book!* 🩶

**Beagle Diner Cozy Mysteries**
Beagles Love Cupcake Crimes
Beagles Love Steak Secrets

Join my newsletter to receive the bonus epilogue and new releases!

The frosting bag shot from Lyra's hand to land smack on the head of her beagle, where a line of frosting now dripped between caramel-colored eyes. In the blink of those eyes, a long tongue wiped off half the mess.

Lyra St. Claire was in her happy place and unprepared when her assistant, Maggie Parker, burst into the Portland Hotel suite she often leased.

"Lucky that wasn't chocolate frosting, Mags. Where's the fire?" Lyra stooped to snatch the bag from the furry head. Not that Cinnamon was bothered by that or her sticky fur. The adorable pooch loved cupcakes which was why she sat hopefully at Lyra's feet during the whole process.

The mainly white dog had a brown back, as if a dusting of cinnamon had been poured along her from head to tail. At least the color had been more that shade as a pup. Now her coat was paler—more of a biscuit shade, really—but it was too late to rue that. Besides, Cinnamon sounded far better than Biscuit.

When Lyra looked up again, Maggie was leaning on the kitchen counter. "You're very pale, Mags. Are you ill?"

Maggie shook her head. "I wish there was a right way to tell you this. There's been an accident at the contestants' hotel."

"Did someone get burned?" That would make perfect sense, as it was a cooking contest that Lyra was judging in Boise, and burns were unfortunately frequent in her profession. "Please tell me they're okay."

"If only I could." Maggie grimaced. "Justine Long fell from her balcony. She's dead."

Lyra gasped. "Oh my goodness. Do you know how it happened?"

Maggie shook her head again. "She went back to her room after a practice session. The police are there, but it will take them some time to talk to everybody."

"The rest of the contestants will be in shock. I should get back there and make sure they're okay."

"Your agent was the one who contacted me. Symon also said to make sure you stayed in Portland. According to him, the police will stop by later. I'm sorry, he didn't give me any more details."

Lyra frowned. "Symon phoned you? Why didn't he contact me?"

Maggie screwed up her nose. "I was surprised too. The contestant's hotel manager called the producer, and he called Symon. Your agent might not have bothered to come on this trip, but you know how tuned in he is to everything that's going on."

Lyra knew exactly what Maggie meant. Symon's finger was firmly on the pulse of every detail of her career—whether she wanted it or not. He should have called her himself, but she couldn't deny it was a relief not to have him around when his presence upset everyone. Including Cinnamon.

Full of reasons for what he expected of her while

ignoring her suggestions, she'd bet a strawberry cheesecake he already knew exactly what had happened but was thinking of damage control and not Justine, her family, or the other contestants.

She dialed Symon's number, which clicked to voice mail almost immediately. Clearly she wouldn't get any information from him until he was good and ready, but she desperately needed to know more. She was involved whether he liked it or not, and felt responsible for all the contestants' well-being.

Lyra was well-known as a celebrity chef, and her TV show, *A Lesson with Lyra*, featured guests who were also celebrities. Her platform was the girl-next-door who could teach anyone to cook recipes packed with flavor.

She also hosted regional cooking contests. Boise was the last one and the competition was fierce. After that, the winners of each leg would appear in a grand final held here in Portland. She'd unfortunately had to make the extra trips back and forth to do various pre-show promotions.

Lyra snatched up a cloth and wiped the counter vigorously. "This is tragic. She was so talented, and destined to do well, but I can admit to you that I wasn't particularly fond of Justine. Her abrasive personality made her unpopular with everyone, and sometimes she was downright cruel. I personally witnessed her 'accidentally' knocking other contestants' dishes over on more than one occasion and had to step in." Lyra paused, cloth in hand. "Surely, another contestant didn't have anything to do with her death?"

Maggie frowned. "Do you mean is this a did she fall or was she pushed scenario?"

"Exactly. Because I can't believe Justine would take her own life when she had so much to live for." The words came out a little shaky. "If there was an argument and Justine lost her footing—that's one thing. But what if that wasn't the case?"

"Wow. You think someone wanted retribution? I guess anything's possible." Maggie let that sink in before adding, "We're back there in a few days for the final. I'm sure you'll know more by then either via the papers or if Symon gets in contact."

The counter couldn't be any cleaner, and, needing something to do, Lyra finished frosting the last of the cupcakes. "That's true, although, if it was foul play, they might cancel the rest of the contest."

Leaning over the tray, Maggie followed each swirl with fascination. "They never have after an accident. Then again, no one died before."

"Thank goodness. But however the death happened, it will be hard for the rest of them to continue." Lyra shook her head at her assistant. "I don't know how you can eat, but help yourself. I'll make coffee."

"Food makes me feel better when I'm upset." Maggie grabbed a cupcake and sniffed in appreciation. "Mmmm, chocolate."

Lyra couldn't argue with the reasoning. "Chocolate with a twist. Made especially for you."

Cinnamon, now miraculously clean, padded around the counter to Maggie for a scratch, big eyes glued to the cupcake.

"Poor Cin. I'd give you some if I was allowed."

"She knows she can't have chocolate. Although, it doesn't stop her from wishing I'd drop more than the frosting."

Lyra made coffee, and they sat companionably at the counter.

"These are so good." Maggie nonchalantly reached for a second cupcake.

"I knew you'd love the caramel center, but perhaps you could save one or two for Dan."

Her driver, who did anything else required, would be here soon, and he loved all of Lyra's baking. Between these two, she had discerning taste testers on hand whenever she needed them, and, along with Cinnamon, they took her mind off the troubles which had lately escalated.

Maggie reached for a napkin and dabbed her mouth, the beagle still at her feet in case a few crumbs happened her way. Suddenly, Cinnamon ran to the door, and then a knock sounded. It was Maggie who checked the peephole and admitted the police while Lyra calmed her nerves by wiping the counter some more and making a fresh pot of coffee.

Maggie had done her best to take Lyra's mind off Justine, but if she were honest, she'd barely been distracted. There were so many unanswered questions, and she hoped the officers had answers.

## 2

R eturning to Boise was hard, but necessary. The mercifully short flight took them over the small-town of Fairview which had once been her home. Lyra peered out the window to catch a glimpse. Though she hadn't been back in years, and lived in a lavish apartment in LA, a part of her would always miss the familiar crisscross of roads, the lake, and sense of peace that had been lacking since she left.

As soon as they landed her driver collected the delivered limousine and took them straight to the contestant's hotel. It wasn't super fancy, but, as Lyra could attest, when you were young and struggling to find your way, a hotel that had working elevators and clean towels every day was amazing.

Not all the contestants fit into the financially challenged category. Justine Long certainly didn't, and, according to Lyra's agent, her parents were out for retribution. Maybe they deserved it, but from whom or what, no one seemed to know, which made things doubly upsetting—and awkward.

The police believed Justine committed suicide, so Symon sent her into the fray to do damage control. He played to her weakness of caring and wanting to make things right with the excuse that he was too busy.

*Too busy to do his job?* Lyra swallowed her anger and slipped out of the cab after Maggie. None of this was the contestants' fault, and she worried how it was affecting them.

Nodding to the concierge, who was expecting them, they hurried to the elevator and rode it to the next floor. Maggie had arranged for the manager to let them use the conference room so Lyra could speak to the contestants together.

Some were tearful, while others paced the room, but they were all there. "Thanks so much for coming this morning. I know Justine's death is a terrible thing to come to terms with, and I'm proud of you for not quitting." She looked at each of them, having already decided to be completely honest no matter that Symon had told her what to say. "You have every right to be upset by this and what the media are reporting about it not being an accident, despite what the police say."

A dark-haired contestant sat at a table chewing her nails. "They don't know for certain that it wasn't," she muttered.

"Do you know something that would prove there was foul play, Ashley? This is important. I don't want anyone else to get hurt, and I'm sure you don't either," Lyra implored.

Ashley's mouth quivered. "I only know what we all do. Justine bagged you the whole time. She was jealous of anyone who got more airtime than her, but she truly couldn't stand you."

Lyra grimaced. The police might find that interesting, and she wondered what Ashley had told them. "Do you know why?"

"Isn't it obvious? You have everything she wanted and was determined to get no matter how many people she had to step on."

Lyra's skin prickled. "Did she do anything about her dislike of me?"

"Ashley, you don't have any proof," Cameron Willett gently admonished his fellow contestant. Older than the rest but younger than Lyra, he was a favorite because of his kindness. Always looking out for the ones who struggled, he'd never had a cross word with any of them, as far as she knew.

"Maybe not," Ashley continued, "but we all know it was Justine who let that paparazzi guy onto the set when Lyra banned him."

"That is true," he admitted.

Lyra's mouth was suddenly dry. "You mean Duane Buchanan?"

Ashley nodded. "The day after that, there was a write-up on Justine and how she was the favorite to win."

Lyra's heart hardened. This was no coincidence. Since she banned him against her agent's wishes, which hadn't been easy, Duane was always looking for ways to attack Lyra, and spreading false information was his favorite way to do that. Still, killing a contestant had to be a step too far to get at her. Didn't it?

"Then there was the day your soufflé flopped. Before you came on set, I saw her do something to your flour." Ashley's lip wobbled. "I'm sorry I didn't say anything, but she threatened me."

"That's my fault," Cameron said quietly. "When Ashley told me what she'd seen and that Justine knew, I thought if she stayed quiet, Justine might leave her alone."

It took an effort to continue as normal so as not to upset the group more than they were. "Justine was particularly rough on you, Ashley. I should have stepped in, and I'm sorry for that."

The young woman sniffed. "I know you tried, and I

understand that the producers love all that stuff for the ratings. I just wanted to get through until the end despite her dislike of me. I certainly never harmed her."

"No one thinks that."

Ashley's shoulders slumped. "The questions the police asked sure made it sound like they did."

"Justine wasn't liked by any of us, but we don't think she'd kill herself. She was too intent on beating us and gloating." Cameron paled. "The rest of us are worried, because if she didn't throw herself off the building, who did?"

The other contestants nodded anxiously. Clearly they had discussed this at length and were on the same page. Scared by what this could mean, naturally they wanted to know more—just as she did. While Lyra agreed that it was unlikely a young woman with everything pointing to a standout career as a chef would kill herself, she couldn't encourage them to do more than stay in the competition. Searching for answers might put them in danger.

"I hear what you're saying, but the police have decided it was death by misadventure. Therefore, the producers can resume. The kitchen will be open tomorrow, and I've ordered more security until the final episode because of the paparazzi. Please continue to practice, even though I appreciate it will be hard. You're a great team, and you will get through this."

"I don't know how you live like this." Ashley sniffed again. "The press and the studio all yelling and giving orders scares me."

"Unfortunately, it comes with the territory," Lyra admitted. "But it's not all bad. I get to spend time with people such as yourselves, and I love that."

Cameron put his arm around Ashley's shoulder. "We'll be all right. I'll look after you."

Lyra swallowed hard. "Is everybody else okay?"

The group nodded with little enthusiasm.

Cameron smiled gently. "As upset as we are, we won't let you down, Ms. St. Claire."

"Thank you—all of you. Spending so much time together, I'm sure this tragedy affects you all more than the rest of us involved. If anyone needs to talk, you can contact me or this grief counselor."

Cameron took the cards she offered and handed them to the others. Sadly, it appeared to be something they would all consider.

"One last thing. I have a surprise for you. Tonight, you're having dinner in this room, and you don't have to lift a finger. If you can, take a little time out of your grief to enjoy the meal and one another's company."

That cheered them up a little, which helped Lyra face her next task—speaking to Justine's parents. They were meeting in a suite upstairs, and only one thing made this a little easier —Maggie and Cinnamon were coming with her.

Lyra called them in for a few minutes so Cinnamon could say hi to the contestants. They loved the beagle, and by the time Lyra left, the mood seemed less somber. But in the elevator, after Lyra explained to Maggie what had been said, she was back to needing answers to why Justine had taken her life or who might have orchestrated her death.

Maggie knocked on the door and Mr. Long opened it. He was pale except for the red around his eyes. When they entered, Maggie made Cinnamon stay with her while Lyra continued further into the room to where Justine's parents now stood by the floor-to-ceiling windows. Mrs. Long's cheeks were tearstained and she glared at Lyra.

"Thank you for seeing me. I want to say how sorry I am for your loss. We all are."

Mr. Long snorted. "I find that hard to believe when the competition is proceeding with no respect for our daughter."

Lyra privately agreed but wasn't successful in swaying the producers. "It was a hard decision to make, but we're so far through already, and the other contestants wish to continue—"

"Of course they would now that their biggest threat is gone," Mrs. Long interrupted tartly.

Since the other contestants couldn't hear this, Lyra let the hurtful words slide off her. "Justine was very talented, like so many of the others."

"She was better than every one of them and every bit as good as you, but that's not the point." Mrs. Long clutched at a silk scarf around her neck. "Our child was left in your care, and now she's gone."

"I appreciate that Justine may have been struggling in this environment, but she never mentioned any issues, and I wasn't aware of any. If I had known, I would have made sure she had help."

"I refuse to believe our daughter killed herself," her father began, "but if she did, it was due to the stress, and you should have noticed that. We're going to sue you."

"I'm sorry you feel that I'm to blame, Mr. Long. Please let us know the details of Justine's funeral. I'm sure some of the people attached to the show will wish to come."

"As if we would want any of them there. The way my daughter was treated is shameful, and each of you is just as guilty as the next."

Lyra chewed her bottom lip for a second. "I don't think me being here is doing any good. Again, I'm so sorry. Please feel free to use the room for as long as you like. All expenses are taken care of."

"So they should be," Mr. Long muttered, and his wife began to sob.

Cinnamon whined as they left the couple and waited for the elevator.

"I'm sorry you didn't get to use your magic, Cin," Lyra murmured. "They're hurting too much right now to let you try."

The beagle tilted her head as if weighing that up.

"You handled that as best you could," Maggie assured her. "They wouldn't even look at me, and I didn't feel I could add anything anyway."

"Nothing either of us could say would have made a difference. They need to blame someone, and it's natural that they see me as the person who should have protected Justine."

Maggie pursed her lips. "No other celebrity would front up the way you have. Symon should have been the one dealing with this. Or the producers. Between them they could have found someone to take the heat off you."

"You're not wrong, Mags, but I still would have felt obliged to see Justine's parents. It's my name on the show, and I feel a responsibility for what happens on it."

"I know, but you didn't hurt the girl, and if she'd been on any other show, Justine would have been given the boot a month ago for the things she said and did."

Lyra nodded but couldn't shake the feeling that she should have done something when the other incidents happened. Her recipes were perfected before she made them in public, so when one failed, it was not only rare but there had to be a reason that had nothing to do with her. Only, how could she have proven that without causing a huge disruption and upsetting all the contestants? "I'll be glad when this leg of the contest is over and we can move on to the grand finale in Portland. These heats have been more exhausting than any I remember."

"With so much going wrong, I'm not surprised you're exhausted. I'll be glad to get home too." Maggie peered into the lobby as soon as they reached the ground floor. "There's a bunch of reporters outside, and I'm sure one is Duane Buchanan." She signaled to the concierge, and he hurried over. "Could you take us out another entrance, please?" she asked him.

"Certainly." He led them down a hall and swiped his card at the door. "Do you have a car?"

"Yes, I've messaged the driver. Thank you."

Once outside, Lyra sucked in the fresh air before they rushed to the end of the building where her driver waited. It wasn't until they were on their way that she relaxed into the seat. The familiar warmth of Cinnamon leaning against her was reassuring and settled her thoughts.

She turned to face her assistant. "I have to do something, Mags. Mainly for the other contestants, but I can't live with myself if I ignore everything and something else happens. The tragedy will follow them until the show finishes, but after this heat, there's still the final to get through for the rest of us."

"Tell me how I can help."

Maggie didn't hesitate, which made Lyra smile. "I'm going to investigate this myself. Symon will hit the roof if he finds out, so I'd like you to run interference whenever possible."

"No problem as long as you promise to stay safe."

"I promise. If I could shut the show down, I would, but Symon won't hear of it."

Maggie snorted. "Did you imagine he would? It's all about the money for him."

Lyra nodded. Symon wouldn't risk them being sued no matter what she said.

She'd never felt as trapped as she did right now by the job

she loved, and the craving for her small hometown of Fairview was growing every day. Or maybe she'd simply been pretending all this time that living a high-pressured existence in LA, and on the road, didn't get to her anymore.

## 3

A month later, Lyra's stomach gave that familiar swirl when she peered out of the elevator. Maggie stood at the hotel lobby door and beckoned her. With the assurance that she wasn't about to get mobbed, Lyra wrapped the diamond-encrusted leash around her hand and hurried across the foyer with one nosy beagle.

The doorman tipped his hat as they stepped outside into the sunshine of spring in Portland, and a camera went off in her face. Blinded for a second, Lyra couldn't see who was behind it and stumbled down a step, gripping the leash of her frightened beagle.

Maggie caught Lyra's arm and managed to keep her upright. Her driver appeared on her other side, and between them, they bundled her into her limousine.

Maggie thrust Cinnamon on Lyra's lap and climbed in beside her. "Get us out of here, Dan."

They pulled away from the curb with a squeal of tires, and Lyra turned in time to catch a glimpse of a man in a dark trench coat. Coal black eyes stayed with her on the drive. Not the color—the hatred in them. She shouldn't be shocked.

Duane Buchanan turned up everywhere she went sooner or later.

Maggie groaned. "I'm really sorry about that, Lyra. I swear I checked every doorway up and down for thirty feet, and Dan stayed to make sure it remained clear while I went inside to get you."

Lyra nodded. Dan was extremely careful, and he'd be upset that Duane had slipped by him. "I know you both did your best. Paparazzi don't play by the same rules as the rest of the world."

"Never knowing when they'll pop out of the woodwork is driving me crazy, and it's not just that." Maggie huffed. "After the incident in Boise, Symon promised to be around to cover all contingencies. I wish you'd find another agent, or at least hire a bodyguard."

She'd been saying the same thing for several months, and each time, Lyra felt the truth of her words a little deeper. Especially after Boise.

All the work she'd done to find the reason Justine died came to nothing. Every contestant insisted Justine was determined to win the competition at all costs, and they all had accounts of threats and interference by her. Since she always appeared so confident, and happy to be in the limelight, nothing indicated Justine was suicidal.

Lyra also spoke to everyone at the hotel involved with the group, including the concierge and cleaners. They'd already been interviewed by the police and had nothing to add about strangers around the contestants or seeing anything out of place.

She should have been mollified, but Lyra had a lingering fear that somehow, she was to blame. No matter that her agent told her she was being dramatic, she couldn't shake the idea that someone wanted to hurt her and, unable to do so, had vented their frustration on an innocent bystander.

When Symon found out she was asking questions, he was furious. It didn't stop her, but with no leads, she had to let it go for the sake of the contestants, who were over the scrutiny. It was hard to continue with the heat, but in the end, Cameron Willett was crowned the winner, and the rest of the group seemed happy about that. He made a great speech, thanking Lyra for his opportunity, and mentioned Justine's talent.

Now she was back in Portland to cover the finals, and her anxiety was through the roof. All the finalists were clearly talented, but would their aspirations outweigh their sense of fair play, or was she barking up the wrong tree?

"I'll deal with the security issue when we get home, Mags. I promise." Tackling Symon about anything was like walking a tightrope and never pleasant. While he'd done a lot for her, Symon dropped the ball too many times. Constantly unreachable, and with security faltering more with each trip, it was time to have a reckoning. Maggie was right—it was long overdue.

"I'm holding you to that, because quite frankly, I'm scared for you," Maggie pressed. "You've had recipes go wrong, and valuable gifts have disappeared. Last week you were almost run down, a week prior there was the electrical fault in your restaurant, and now this. You could have broken something if you'd fallen down the rest of those steps."

"There are plenty of logical reasons for what happened. The electrical issue might have been lack of maintenance, and I didn't get more than a couple of scrapes with that car business. The stumble was caused by a photographer's flash. All those could be bad luck or coincidence."

Maggie raised an eyebrow. "You don't believe that, and neither do I."

Lyra sighed, and Cinnamon, who'd been watching attentively, nosed her cheek. Maggie didn't mention the death of

Justine Long. In between the Boise competition and the finals, they'd gone home to LA and the subject was barely raised. It also hadn't appeared again in the papers after the first wave of headlines and was as if it hadn't happened. This made her sad and wary. Symon had a lot of sway with the media, but how far did it extend?

Mentally shaking herself, Lyra knew she couldn't dwell on this now. It was time to focus solely on today's competition, and that meant keeping things positive no matter how she felt.

Luckily, they were at their destination and Portland had turned on a great day. First out of the limo, Maggie stood opposite the door as a shield in case the press had been alerted. Dan chose to stay away from the obvious entrances of the show, and that had clearly worked. The limousine alone attracted attention, and even with her scarf pulled up high, Lyra ran the risk of being spotted. Symon always insisted she play the part of a star, from her makeup and clothes to where she stayed and how she arrived in each city.

Having Cinnamon with her was another huge giveaway, but they were a duo and rarely out of each other's sight, so Lyra accepted long ago that privacy hung on a knife edge. That didn't mean she had to make it easy for the paparazzi.

Lyra emerged, followed by Cinnamon, who stepped by them to look up and down the street like the good watchdog she was. "Is it safe, girl?"

"Woof!"

Lyra grinned at her sweet girl, who was arguably as famous as she was. "I'll take that as a yes."

"Are you sure you'll be okay from here?" Dan asked.

He'd already scouted the area and the setup but hated to leave anything to chance.

"We'll be fine. Everyone will be around the corner where the stage is, and that's where they'll expect me to come from."

She knew he watched them for a while before he drove the limousine back down the tree-lined boulevard, and it made her smile. The three of them bypassed the mayor's offices, which were attached to the courthouse. They rounded the corner where the imposing building showed off its century or two of architectural elegance to the best advantage.

Maggie led her between the buildings and into the cordoned-off area behind the tent. She was hardly onto the walkway when a woman screamed at her from behind the velvet rope.

"Lyra, Lyra. I love you!"

This set off a chain reaction around the crowd, and a flush crept up her cheeks, which was silly when she'd been treated to this level of adoration consistently for the last few years. A trainee chef plucked from obscurity and turned into a TV show host, Lyra was still in awe that so many people loved her style of cooking and, by default, her.

The concept of taking the ordinary and making it restaurant quality had grabbed her imagination from the time she first learned to cook as a child with her mom showing her the basics.

"Thank you," she said, her voice drowning in the sea of other shouts, while cameras flashed in her eyes and a reporter shoved a microphone at her face, just missing her nose.

"Let's save our questions until after the presentation." Maggie ran interference, pulling Lyra to the side and through a gap into a large white tent. "Whew! It never gets any easier to get past them."

"I'd be a nervous wreck if it wasn't for you, Maggie. I swear some of them would take a piece of me if they could." Lyra ran her fingers through the long red waves of hair released from the scarf. Photographers and news crews weren't too fussy with what they chose to show, and she was just vain enough not to want to look a complete mess.

When the local television station sent someone down to the Portland cookery school she attended four years ago, she was one of a class of sixteen and in her third year of training. Unaware of the visitor in the room—a well-known producer of cooking shows—until he began to watch her closely and ask questions, her focus was entirely on filling the tortellini she'd made.

Being literally in the right place at the right time, her signature dish from that day, crispy salmon with a miso-dressed salad, had come along for the ride. The ratings proved that from the pilot, and after that, the show became a runaway success.

With work as her focus and no other distraction, she'd written four cookbooks she was proud of and opened her restaurant, La Joliesse, six months ago. Pronounced "jo-lee-ES," the name came from the French word for grace and loveliness. This was her greatest achievement and came a close second only to her love of Cinnamon.

Lyra sat in the chair she'd been directed to so the makeup artist could touch up her face. Cinnamon made this a little awkward, since she insisted on lying under the chair, where she didn't exactly fit, and every time she moved, the chair rocked.

Just as the makeup was done, a runner poked her head around the door opening, startling the beagle, who banged her head for the tenth time.

"Ms. St. Claire, there's a group of six children from the local school who'd like to present you with flowers at the end. Would you mind?"

"Tell Maggie who they are so she can get security to let them through if they're not part of the paid group, then send them up on stage before I finish."

"They haven't paid, and since it's a sellout, there's no room. The guests might get antsy if they have to squash up anymore," the runner said, hopping from one foot to the other. "They're happy to wait outside the tent."

Her sympathy for the children was touching. Symon would have cut off any suggestion that plans should change. Since he wasn't here, the decision was an easy one.

"Bring them up on stage now and have them sit on the far side. They can hand me the flowers at the end and watch the show for free."

The runner gasped. "Thanks so much, Ms. St. Claire. They adore you, and I know they'll be thrilled at the opportunity to see you up close."

Lyra shared a smile with Maggie, who understood Lyra's need to impassion everyone with cooking, especially children.

For the next few minutes, Lyra mentally went over the speech she was making today while Maggie studied her clipboard and checked off all the elements of the show that she oversaw.

A hand touched her shoulder, making Lyra jump slightly.

"You're on," Maggie said softly.

Taking a deep breath, Lyra stood. "Come on, Cinnamon. It's showtime."

Cinnamon's head gave the folding chair another thump, and she threw the world an accusatory look as she eased her way out with difficulty. Considering how smart her dog was, the way Cinnamon consistently squeezed into too-small spaces—and always with the same result—made Lyra laugh.

This was the best medicine and a great way to start the show.

4

————————

Maggie led them from behind the canvas door, and Lyra was back in the bright sunlight. Her sunglasses were in her bag, but she wouldn't use them, as much as it would be a relief. Intent on making a connection with her fans, she understood that they liked to look in her eyes and know she saw them too.

One thing she'd learned in this mad life she called her career was that no matter how famous a person might be, they didn't stay that way if they didn't show up and give the fans what they wanted. Social media had a lot to do with being accessible, but there was no substitute for the real thing. It was a balancing act of being grateful to her fans and keeping something of herself back to retain her sanity, but the scales often leaned in one direction more than the other.

A round of applause accompanied more shrieking of her name—and Cinnamon's. She smiled, waved, and made eye contact with as many as she could. Cinnamon barked to announce her presence, trotting along and wagging her tail at all the excitement buzzing around them. Then they were at the podium. The crowd settled down, and on cue, Cinnamon flopped at Lyra's feet.

"Good morning. Thank you so much for coming to this wonderful event. I'm honored to have been one of the judges and appreciate that you've been waiting a while, so I won't talk too much before we move on to the fun stuff."

A few laughs ensued.

"As you know, I'm here for two purposes. Firstly, to announce the winner of the best new junior chef in Portland, and secondly, to open the children's competition. As you see, we have eight stations set up to your left, where our young contestants are ready to show how they got here by cooking their signature dishes. One finalist each will be chosen from the savory and sweet categories."

Heads turned to face the children, who wore expressions ranging from scared witless to overly excited and everything in between. Lyra knew the feeling too well, having been only twenty-three years old when she'd been plucked from her training and thrown into the deep end of celebrity status. It was heady stuff, even now at twenty-seven. At twelve to fourteen years of age, she imagined it would be even more of a culture shock for all but the hardiest of these young contestants.

She'd met each of them and watched them in the earlier rounds, which were held in the studio's headquarters in Portland. They'd touched her heart with their earnestness and, in some cases, bravado. Each one impressed her in different ways, but they were all so focused—something she could also relate to. As far as she was concerned, the best contribution she could give them—apart from helping with the jump into fame, if that was the way it went—was to make sure they had fun while they cooked.

Her joy at producing every dish the way she imagined it should be was only one aspect of what the TV executives were looking for. Flair and a connection with the audience also mattered. On one hand, while the flair had been easy because of her passion, she'd had to work hard to feel comfortable talking about her recipes and explaining the process to a camera—let alone a group of people, or person-to-person on a stage.

Lyra also believed she had a responsibility to help people appreciate a diverse and healthy palate. Her mom had grown their own vegetables and fruit back in Fairview, and freshness had never been an issue. As she got older, Lyra noticed that her friends ate from packets or had takeout more often than not. That was an eye-opener, which she and her mom had talked about at length. Everyone made their choices, but sometimes it was out of a lack of understanding.

Lyra shook her head to bring herself back to the present. It was to Portland where everything had begun that made her feel whimsical. Even though her mom lived in LA now, their history was in that small town not so far away, when Portland had been their only big city experience.

"We'll introduce all of them to you very soon, but now let's get back to the winner of Best Junior Chef."

She looked down to the first row, where the eight adult contestants sat. While not as openly nervous as the children sitting several feet away, she recognized the signs—folded arms, eyes down, fidgeting, wringing of hands, eyes glued to her as though she might toss them a clue. This was one of those moments that could make a huge difference in a person's life, which made her feel elated for the winner yet sad for the others who had tried so hard. The winner from Boise, Cameron Willett, gave her a hopeful smile, as did all the other winners from around the country.

Seeing the disappointment of all but one was always hard, yet there was nothing she could do about it. She forced herself to smile back, then turned to the wings. Nodding to the technician, the tent behind them became a large screen, and eight dishes stood out on the whiteness of the canvas. Lyra called out the name of each one, and the chef responsible came onto the stage.

"You've all done exceptionally well, which made it very difficult for Mayor Clements, Suki Love, and me to decide who truly deserved the title. As you know, there can only be one winner, but I'd like to congratulate you all for getting to this stage."

A hush descended as Suki, a beautiful rising movie star and another local export, brought out an envelope that Lyra slit open.

"The prize, including production of your own cookbook, a guest appearance on *A Lesson with Lyra,* and an all-expenses-paid cruise for two, goes to… Adam Lancaster!"

The crowd went crazy as Lyra handed Adam a larger envelope with his tickets inside, plus a Perspex and gold trophy of a chef's hat with his name emblazoned on its base along with the accolade of Best Young Chef of the Year.

"Well done." She held out her hand.

Adam ignored the hand, grabbed her shoulders, and kissed her firmly on the lips.

Confusion and annoyance fought with each other as she pushed him away. Flashing cameras amid several wolf whistles captured that moment forever. Her professionalism ensured she didn't make a fuss, but she would be having stern words with Adam Lancaster when they were done here.

Cinnamon growled at the young man, and Lyra moved as far as she could from the hubbub of the other contestants as they congratulated him. The crowd, up on their feet, enthusiastically cheered for the handsome chef.

The decision was unanimous, which Lyra had no qualms about since Adam deserved to win. The only problem, and it was a doozy, was that Adam was a pain in the neck. Early on during the competition, he'd decided that by sticking near Lyra, he would always appear before any other contestant, and if the media thought there was something more between them, so much the better.

The truth he conveniently dismissed was that each contestant had one-on-one time with her. The exposure on this one was initiated by a TV executive, who thought they looked good together and pimped it out to push the ratings. Naturally, the other contestants were not amused and Lyra made sure she was never alone with him again, which didn't stop him from flirting every chance he could.

Plastering a smile on her face, she calmed her exasperation and growing dislike with a few deep breaths. Adam knew exactly what he'd done. Photos would appear with or without her consent, because that was how the celebrity game worked, and there wasn't a darn thing she could do about it.

She took a few minutes to commiserate with the other finalists. Lyra hated this part. No matter how brave they were, there was no denying that all of them were disappointed. Nothing she could say would fix that, but the words came anyway. "It really was so close."

"Like you said, there can only be one winner," Cameron said with a smile. "No one blames you, and we know we tried our best, right, guys?"

The others nodded, and not for the first time, she wished she could help them all. Luckily, they were a tight bunch and had Cameron to cheer them up.

"You sure did. Now, don't forget to celebrate getting this far, and good luck to all of you in the future." Lyra shook their hands before she turned away.

When she looked for Maggie and Cinnamon, something drew her attention. Actually, *someone*. A man stood alone to the left of the area as the crowd began to migrate to the cordon around the children. He was staring at her. This was nothing new, but there was something familiar about him. The cropped fair hair and the way he stood—hands deep in his pockets. He was also unsmiling, which made her look again.

*Kaden Hunter?*

It couldn't be. Her good friend had always had a ready smile for her over the years.

Then a ray of light bounced off the marquee, revealing that it really was him. Her heart skipped a beat. *What is he doing here?* It had been four years since they'd worked side by side at chef training school. Both from the Portland area, they'd also done some practical work in local restaurants and spent hours together testing recipes and studying. Did he remember her?

Her heart did a happy dance as memories flooded her. Then she was mobbed by the VIP group, who expected handshakes and free signed cookbooks. She stood on tiptoes to give him a tentative wave, and he returned a brief nod before she was swallowed up.

So, he did know it was her. They hadn't spoken for so long that she didn't have a clue what he'd been up to and didn't have time to find out.

Lyra signed books and anything else put in front of her as well as shaking so many hands it made her a little dizzy. Finally, she was whisked over to the children's area, where it was her job to introduce them all.

She loved watching the children, empathizing with their need to make things slightly different than the norm and hoping to make them feel more at ease. When she thought they couldn't wait another second, she waved the green flag an assistant gave her.

"Okay, it's time to begin. Let's get this show cooking!"

A clamor began as the children pulled out their pots and pans and other appliances, and she glanced back once more to where Kaden had stood. The space his six-foot-three frame had filled was replaced with someone much shorter.

She knew him too, but not as favorably. Duane Buchanan looked her up and down, then glared at her. A shiver ran down her back. This man scared her.

"Are you okay?" Maggie whispered.

The shine had fallen from the day, but Lyra wouldn't give him the power to ruin it completely. He and the cold-eyed Kaden Hunter needed to lighten the heck up and leave her alone. "I'm fine. I better go watch the kids."

"I'll take Cinnamon." Maggie held her hand out.

Lyra reluctantly handed her the leash. The beagle grounded her, but no matter how well-behaved Cinnamon was, she couldn't walk around the kitchen.

Then again, neither could the paparazzi.

## 5

Lyra wearily walked with Maggie from the hotel to the restaurant district. In the opposite direction from the courthouse, she hoped to fly under the radar of any fans. Changing clothes and her coat, Lyra hid her hair under a different scarf. At Dan's insistence, they left by a side door.

Thankfully the roads were clear, because she was famished. Tasting all the contestants' food was the sum of everything Lyra ate that day, and she was looking forward to a proper meal from a restaurant the mayor suggested. His daughter was getting married tomorrow and having her reception there. Apparently this restaurant had been around for about a year and was still heavily booked most nights. Along with the mayor's recommendation, this spoke volumes, and Maggie was adept at scoring reservations without dropping Lyra's name unless it was necessary.

A loud clang startled her from her thoughts, and she swung around to see a man picking up a sign that had fallen. He seemed familiar but was too far away and headed in the other direction to see him better.

"You're not still thinking about Duane, are you?"

Her assistant was far too intuitive, and Lyra tried to sound casual. "Why do you ask?"

Maggie flicked back her hair. "I saw your face when you noticed him."

"I hope no one else did. He brings out the worst in me."

"Oh, please. You're nothing but polite to everyone, including that creep who doesn't deserve it. I can only imagine what he's going to print about you tomorrow."

"There's nothing we can do to change that, but if you could hear my thoughts, you'd run a mile."

Maggie laughed. "I bet they aren't worse than mine. Want to share?"

"Let's not spoil the evening. Besides, I prefer thinking about food."

"Thank goodness." Maggie rubbed her stomach. "I could eat a horse and chase the rider."

They laughed again and picked up the pace as dusk fell around them. It was pretty in this part of Portland. Fairy lights decorated the trees along the main roads toward the restaurants, and she loved the festive atmosphere.

Cinnamon would have loved it too, but Lyra had left her at the hotel. Most top restaurants had no outside dog area, and coincidently over the afternoon, the beagle proved unable to resist too many tidbits from the well-meaning audience members and contestants in between breaks. Tonight, Cinnamon was lethargic and happy to stay in her comfy bed.

An empty building drew her attention. "Maggie, wait up a minute."

Her assistant sighed, used to Lyra and her need to consider any location as a place to open another restaurant. It became a habit two years ago, and she simply couldn't resist the urge.

Opening a second restaurant here not far from her home-town of Fairview was a dream of Lyra's, but right now she had enough to cope with, so this was more a case of wishful thinking.

Once she found the perfect spot to open La Joliesse in LA, it had taken her a year to be happy with the plans and another four months to get the building fitted out. Every spec was lovingly researched, with each space designed for a particular task.

The opening had been a star-studded affair, and her agent, who'd been introduced to her as soon as she arrived in Los Angeles, had found a wonderful new photographer for the event. Shy, compassionate, and intelligent, Emilia Corban produced an amazing spread of pictures for a prestigious cooking magazine, using Lyra's status as a celebrity chef tastefully. This gave her fledgling restaurant a massive boost she was grateful for.

"This is it." Maggie pointed at the restaurant across the road.

Extra-tall glass doors showcased the front and made the place look inviting and trendy. This was the first tick of approval for a like-minded business owner.

The maître d' greeted them with a friendly smile as soon as they entered. "Good evening."

"Good evening. We have a booking for Parker, please," Maggie said.

"Certainly, your table is ready. Please, let me take your coats."

From behind Maggie, Lyra slipped off her brown coat and handed it to him, followed by the same-colored scarf. Her slim assistant wore a black coat with a blue pleated skirt teamed with a purple shirt. With her golden skin tone and almost black hair, it was a great look. Being curvier, the style wouldn't suit Lyra, but she was happy with her own green velvet dress, short black boots and matching wide belt.

The distinguished maître d' had no doubt been doing this job for some time. Polite and helpful, he knew how to treat a customer, yet when he turned back to them after hanging their coats, his mouth dropped open.

"I had no idea...."

Lyra put a hand on his arm and said softly, "Please don't make a fuss. We're here for a quiet meal, nothing more. Could you make that happen?"

He glanced behind him toward the kitchen at the far end of the room. His eyes suddenly twinkled; then he nodded and answered just as softly. "Of course, Ms. St. Claire. Right this way. This is our best table," he said proudly when he reached a natural curve in the room. "I hope it is acceptable?"

It was the most secluded spot in the restaurant, and she made a mental note to tip him well. If the food was as good as the service, they were in for a treat.

Lyra smiled when he held her chair out, while Maggie sat down unaided and was already studying the menu. Or pretending to, since her shoulders shook.

Lyra sighed. They'd been together for a couple of years, yet Maggie still found it amusing when people fawned over them while Lyra wished for some anonymity—just a little. *Is there such a thing?*

"Thank you. What do you recommend, Colin?" She read his name from the gold embossed badge on his black shirt.

He stood taller. "The salmon is our signature dish and has fantastic reviews."

"Then I'll have that, please." Lyra had no interest in reading the menu. She liked to taste recommendations, then base her opinions on her own likes.

Maggie sighed. "I'll have the salmon too."

Poor Maggie often had to endure exclusion from conversations as though she didn't exist. It didn't faze the younger woman, but Lyra struggled with embarrassment over it. She certainly didn't feel as though she were better than anyone, plus Maggie was a sweetheart, taking on any role Lyra needed her to fill.

Colin poured water for them, in danger of spilling it as he stared.

"Thank you," Maggie said pointedly.

It took a second before Colin realized what he was doing, and his face reddened, managing to stop just in time. "Would either of you like another beverage?"

Lyra smiled. He was a quick learner, which was another tick for the restaurant.

"A bottle of your best white, please." Lyra didn't have to work tomorrow until she got back to LA. She also had the distinct impression that Colin knew a thing or two about wine, and although she did have favorites, this would be a pleasant opportunity to match good wine and food with little research.

He appeared delighted and gave a small bow as he backed away.

Maggie snorted as soon as he was out of earshot. "Goodness, I was worried he was going to kneel at your feet."

"Stop that. He was doing nothing of the sort."

"It sure looked that way. Great service though." Maggie dropped her voice as Colin came back with the wine and a basket of breadsticks in record time. He solemnly poured a taste in Lyra's glass and waited for approval.

She inhaled the light yet fruity bouquet before taking a sip and running the liquid around her mouth. "That is good."

A grin threatened his composure, and he gave a small cough as he showed her the label once more. It was a local wine, and that pleased Lyra as well.

"Maggie, would you make a note…"

"Already done," her assistant assured her, placing a notebook and pen on the table.

It never ceased to amaze her how Maggie anticipated her every move.

"Your meal will be out soon," Colin said before returning to his position at the front desk.

"Nice restaurant." Maggie jotted in her notebook again. "I like the wood paneling by the bar, and the lightness of the decor makes the place feel bigger than it is."

Lyra shook her head. "You are so wasted working for me. You could do a dozen other things successfully."

Maggie laughed. "I know, but no one would pay me to decorate like you pay me to play with your dog and organize your life. Plus, there's the travel, meeting famous people, eating amazing food, and drinking fantastic wine. Not a bad job—and it makes my sister green with envy."

Lyra laughed while they clinked glasses, wondering if she could ever pay Maggie enough for making her life so stress-free. Having her assistant around most days gave Lyra a feeling of family, something she missed terribly when she was away from her mom.

Although it was vastly different, Maggie and Lyra both had definite dress sense and liked food, white wine, and charity work—especially charities involving animals.

One of the best days of her life was when Lyra met Maggie at the dog shelter where she volunteered while training for a degree in design. They bonded over puppies and recipes, and the rest was history.

The salmon came in record time, and Lyra suspected that her name had been dropped behind the swinging doors. The plate was a vision of color, and Maggie made several approving noises as she ate with relish.

"I don't know why it seems like I haven't had a decent

meal in a while, but this is ridiculously good," Maggie groaned.

"I all but inhaled mine. The schedule we've been on with guest spots, the show, and the new restaurant means we haven't been home to cook in what feels like forever. Mom would be shocked by that." Lyra dabbed at her mouth, enjoying the lack of a fatty aftertaste common with salmon. It had a different flavor to her signature dish and yet was just as good.

Maggie nodded, then gave Lyra a pleading look. "I know we're just finishing, but I heard from the mayor's wife that the desserts here are even better than the mains."

"This I have to see."

Lyra caught Colin's eye, which wasn't difficult since he'd been watching them most of the time while pretending not to. A few heads had peered around the kitchen door, but otherwise there was no fuss, and since they were semi-sheltered from the room by a small bifold screen, the other diners paid them no attention.

Colin was at their side in a flash. "I hope you enjoyed the dish?"

Lyra pointed to their empty plates. "We did. So much so that we'd like your opinion on dessert too."

His chest puffed out. "You can look no further than the Decadence of Chocolate."

"That sounds perfect. Shall we share it, Mags?"

Maggie glared. "No way."

Lyra laughed. "Calm down, it was just a suggestion. Make that two please, Colin."

A grin split his face. "It's a decision I don't think you'll regret."

"Until I get on the scales," Lyra said quietly to Maggie when he'd gone.

Maggie flicked her fingers. "Me too, but we'll walk it off, and you have an amazing figure."

"She's right. You have no need to worry," a deep voice said from behind them, and Lyra swung around, spilling a little wine at the brazen remark.

# 6

Lyra recognized the voice instantly. Kaden Hunter stood beside her. For such a big man, he'd always moved quietly. She'd admired that about him until today. He'd obviously heard the conversation, and she was mortified. Reasonably happy with the way she looked, it wasn't a discussion she cared to have, even if she couldn't stop the media from doing so. There could be a lot of negativities around plus-size female celebrities, and it was good and bad that, as a chef, she somehow got a pass.

"We're having the chocolate dish," she told him stiffly, annoyed that she couldn't think of one witty comment.

His barely there smile didn't reach his eyes. "Decadence of Chocolate is a good choice."

"You've had it?"

He snorted. "Many times."

She looked him over properly. His fair hair was closely cropped, as it had been four years ago. He wore black pants and a white T-shirt. By comparison, she and Maggie were overdressed, and they weren't the only ones. She'd heard the place was swanky, and the other diners were also dressed for the part. Not so with Kaden.

Then again, he'd never placed much stock in his appearance or in other people's opinion of him. She'd always admired that and tried to emulate it, but once she moved to LA, there was an expectation to dress up every day and to care more than ever what people thought of her. That became tiring when you were worried about getting snapped in the same outfit or just as you put food in your mouth.

Suddenly aware that he was studying her too, her cheeks, which had been warm, were now hot as an oven on grill. "Have you eaten?" It came out before she could stop herself.

He raised an eyebrow. "Is that an offer to join you?"

Maggie's head swiveled between the two of them, and Lyra could feel the heat from her face travel down her neck. *Isn't heat supposed to rise?*

"As I said, we're getting dessert, but if you'd like to, I'll have a seat brought over." Lyra was already scanning the restaurant for Colin, who was unfortunately talking to other diners.

"No need." Kaden took a vacant chair from another table and put it next to Lyra.

Again, she looked to Colin, half expecting the maître d' to object if the table next to them was booked and the chair required. It really wasn't her issue, but she liked things to run smoothly and imagined the owner here might feel the same.

She took a deep breath. What could she do about it without causing a scene? Having Kaden so near was making her thought processes slow considerably, but Maggie was giving her an inquiring look.

"Kaden Hunter, this is my assistant and friend, Maggie Parker."

"Delighted." He nodded slightly, his focus fixed on Lyra.

Something in his gaze made her think he knew exactly

how uncomfortable this was making her. Was his intention merely to amuse himself, knowing how she'd react?

Just then, Colin appeared at the table with a glass of red wine and another of water, both for Kaden, which was odd. He also didn't ask if Kaden wanted a menu before leaving again.

"Are you here alone?" she asked, wondering if he was table-hopping.

He shook his head, his mouth twitching in that way he had when he was teasing. "I'm not here to eat."

"But—"

"I heard you were here and thought I'd say hello to a person from my past. Call it curiosity. You must be used to that by now?" He twirled the glass and sniffed appreciatively at the wine before placing it back on the table untouched, then sipped some water.

There was something so dismissive in his tone that it made her skin prickle.

"A person from your past? I thought we were friends."

His eyes narrowed. "I thought so too. However, it was so long ago, I assumed I'd gotten it wrong. In fact, I make it four years since we've seen each other, right?"

Her eyes widened at his tone. "You're angry with me?"

His smile wasn't particularly warm, and he shrugged. "I admit, I was for a while. Actually, I gave you the benefit of the doubt for at least a year, assuming you'd answer my calls eventually, or make one of your own. That should give you a laugh."

Confused, Lyra shook her head at Maggie, who was getting ready to jump to her defense. Kaden wasn't a fan who wanted something from her. He was a good man. He was hurting and somehow blamed her. In doing so, he was also dead wrong, and she wanted—needed—the truth just as much as he apparently did.

43

"Why would I laugh? They had me on a schedule from the first day that was so tight I hardly had time for my mom. I thought you understood how crazy my life got?"

She reached for his hand that was white-knuckling the glass of water, but he moved it away, and her stomach tumbled.

"Yeah, I *understood* for quite some time. A quick call or message to a friend would have obviously made the difference to your success."

Kaden's sarcasm hurt, yet she heard something else in his voice. Sadness? Disappointment?

She leaned forward. "I'm sorry I let you down. It took a while to get my head around everything that happened to me. But you're right, I should have made time for my friends. I'm not really in contact with any of them, but we were best friends. I'm here now, and I really did try to reach you."

He stood, settling his face into a polite mask. "It's good that we both agree you could have tried harder. To be honest, if I couldn't compete for your time then, I imagine it would be far more ambitious to try now. It was good to catch up, and I'm genuinely glad that you've done so well. You look fantastic. Success obviously agrees with you."

While Lyra digested his words, he walked across the room and through the swing doors opposite.

"Wow!" Maggie wasn't so quiet about her thoughts. "He's gorgeous. Who the heck is he, and why was he so upset with you? Surely it can't be about you not calling him?"

Was he gorgeous? Lyra thought him good-looking when they'd been at chef school together, but he'd changed, and she wasn't sure how she felt about that. In the years since she'd seen him, he'd filled out in a good way. His shoulders appeared broader, his arms more muscular. The jeans fit him so well that his long legs were well-defined beneath the firm fabric.

More than that, he seemed surer of himself. But she couldn't remember a time when he got mad at her the way he just did. Frustrated, exhausted, excited—never disappointed or angry. She didn't like that one bit, and it really did hurt.

So, pluses and negatives. Was he still the Kaden who made plans with her in school to open a restaurant because they couldn't imagine working without each other? The hours they'd spent together surely weren't so easy to forget, even though they hadn't managed to reconnect in the intervening years.

With Maggie's eyes drilling into her, Lyra took a thoughtful sip of her wine.

"We studied together until I got the cooking show. We were best friends and called or texted each other when we had a moment, but that was early on after I left. Then life got busy for both of us, I guess, and we lost touch. I wonder what he's doing here?" She played the pain of the meeting down, because if Maggie got wind of it, there would be plenty of questions, and she wasn't up for that.

Maggie gave her a curious look. "In Portland?"

"No, what is he doing in this restaurant?"

"Dishwasher?"

Lyra shook her head. "He's certainly not a dishwasher. Kaden Hunter is a wonderful chef. If no one bat an eye about him going into the kitchen, and since most chefs I know would have a hissy fit if someone barged in, he must be working here in some capacity."

Maggie grimaced. "Yeah, I've seen some of those chefs on our travels and thank my lucky stars every day that you aren't like that."

Lyra snorted, knowing the type of chef she meant—the ones who believed that being gruff, demanding, and rude was the only way to behave. She and Kaden had been determined not to be like that.

C. A. PHIPPS

Her thoughts were interrupted when the desserts arrived.

Colin placed the platters in front of them with a flourish, grinning at their astonishment. "Bon appétit," he said and left them to it.

"Oh my goodness. How are we going to eat a whole one each?" Lyra picked up a spoon. "And where do I start?"

The plate was a vision of five perfectly proportioned but different chocolate tasters. A conical mousse, a square of cake, two truffles—one rolled in coconut, the other in cocoa powder—and a mini tart with raspberries on top.

"Don't hold your breath on my account, and I'm not waiting until you figure it out." Maggie dug her spoon into the mousse. "Although I'd suggest you begin with your favorite in case you run out of room."

Despite the upset of seeing Kaden, it was good advice, and Maggie's straight talking was all Lyra needed to allow herself such an indulgence. Lyra's first choice was also the mousse. She closed her eyes to the exquisite smoothness. Taste and texture—anticipated and delivered. Definitely five stars. She wondered if Kaden had a hand in any of them, because he was amazing with chocolate.

Apart from several moans of ecstasy, they ate in silence until they were done. Colin came back to their table and collected their meticulously clean plates without comment.

"Can I get you anything else?" he asked politely.

Maggie patted her stomach, shaking her head with a rapt smile.

Lyra knew how she felt. "I loved every mouthful, and it was a beautiful end to the meal. May I pay my compliments to the chef, please?"

Colin raised an eyebrow, glancing at the kitchen doors with a frown and giving her request more thought than it should warrant. Being famous, she was often asked to come into the kitchen so she could give her opinion on a course or just to admire the chef's pride in his "perfect" signature dish. She wasn't asking for a tour; it was simply a mark of respect and a little kudos for the chef.

"But didn't you—" Colin cut himself off and smiled. "I'll ask him, right away. I'm sure when he knows it's you, he'll be happy to reconsider."

"That was weird," Maggie voiced Lyra's thoughts when he'd gone. "Chefs love you."

"Maybe the kitchen's understaffed and the chef can't spare me any time." Lyra made excuses while trying to think of another reason for a chef not wanting to see her. Undoubtedly, some were jealous of her quick rise to fame, but she'd never come across one who refused to see her.

Time ticked by with no word from the kitchen. Maggie began to fidget, and Lyra didn't blame her. It had been a long day, and they were both tired, but this was something she felt strongly about.

"We'll give them five more minutes." Lyra folded her hands in her lap and watched the kitchen door.

# 7

Maggie sighed for what seemed like the hundredth time. "He sounds a bit pompous."

"Colin?" Lyra was pondering how the maître d' got on with a chef who didn't like to mix with customers. It was important to have a good relationship with staff at the front of house and also with your customers.

Maggie snorted. "Funny lady. I meant our mysterious chef. All this traveling we do, and we haven't encountered one chef unwilling to show off a little—until now."

Lyra was a little defensive of her fellow chefs. "It's not showing off. Most want to excel with every plate that leaves their kitchen, and they have a right to be proud when they get it perfect. Besides, sharing ideas and recipes helps make us grow as chefs."

"Hmmm." Maggie was barely listening, and she nodded in the direction of Colin. "I believe this chef's response was less than enthusiastic."

Colin dragged his feet as he approached them, less composed than before he'd entered the kitchen.

"I'm sorry, but the chef is not available tonight."

Colin didn't elaborate. In fact, he looked embarrassed, and Lyra was sorry she'd asked. She didn't want to upset the man by pushing the issue further.

"Perhaps another time. I'm sure I'll be back for more of this wonderful food."

Colin smiled with what she assumed was relief.

"Thank you for understanding, Ms. St. Claire. Chef Hunter, as I'm sure you know, is usually more obliging, but he's had a very busy day."

Lyra blinked a couple times as the words hit home. "Pardon? Did you say Chef Hunter? Kaden Hunter is the head chef?" Her voice rose, and several heads turned her way.

Why would Kaden omit that information when it was what he'd always strived for? Confused, she wasn't sure what to think.

"I knew I should have googled him," Maggie muttered as she took out her phone.

Colin blustered for a couple seconds, regarding the door once more. "I assumed he'd told you his position when he stopped by earlier."

Lyra was confused. "I saw him go into the kitchen and assumed he worked here, but I had no idea in what capacity, and he certainly didn't clarify it."

Colin's mouth opened a couple more times, and she tamped down any further recriminations. It wasn't this man's fault, but she wasn't about to leave without finding out why he wasn't bursting to tell an old friend how well he'd done. It was time to play the celebrity card, one she'd never used before. Standing, Lyra turned to Maggie. "Excuse me a moment."

It wasn't easy to gauge Colin's reaction, but Maggie's raised eyebrows as Lyra marched to the kitchen meant there would be some explaining to do. Rushed footsteps from behind made her think Colin may try to stop her, instead he held the left-hand door for her and she stopped just inside.

Kaden, now in his whites, walked between stations. With a commanding presence, he gave firm instructions to his chefs and assistants. The kitchen gleamed. Even with all the things happening at once—sauces being prepared, the grill fired up and sizzling, pots and pans clanging as their variety of ingredients were stirred and tossed—the place was organized and running smoothly. She loved this. The atmosphere called to her, and she barely noticed Colin at her shoulder.

Her presence, as it usually did, sent a ripple around the room when the closest person recognized her and spread the news. She smiled at them until her gaze reached Kaden, who couldn't have looked less happy to see her.

Warily, he came toward her. "What are you doing here? I thought Colin explained?"

While she felt bad for the maître d', Lyra stood her ground. "He did explain that it wasn't possible to meet you. At first, I merely wanted to express how delicious the food was. When I found out you were the head chef here, which you somehow forgot to tell me, it made me want to congratulate you more. And we already know each other, right?"

His gaze was cool. "Head chef? I own Phoenix."

Once upon a time, Lyra would have thrown her arms around him the way they had when one of them achieved something, but if his tone didn't put her off, his stiff body language certainly did.

"That's wonderful news. I didn't know, and I'm so proud for you. It's a beautiful restaurant with gorgeous food."

A flicker in his eyes and a slight pink tinge to his cheeks were the only way she knew the statement affected him.

"Thank you. Is that all?"

Lyra flinched. "You're obviously upset with me, and I

don't want to leave like this. Perhaps we could get together and talk this through when you have time?"

An eyebrow lifted. "What could we possibly need to chat about?"

"Kaden, we haven't seen each other in so long, there must be a million things to talk about. I know I have a lot of questions. Surely you do too?"

He hesitated, and Lyra waited for a no, but he surprised her.

"When did you have in mind?"

"I fly out tomorrow."

The other eyebrow joined its twin. "Then it's not likely, is it?"

Had his easy acceptance been a test? If so, she was failing, which made her panic. "Tonight? After you close." It would be late, but she would happily not sleep if they could clear the air between them.

Kaden was very still, the way he was when making a big decision. "I'm busy tonight."

They stared at each other, his face a mask, hers hot with embarrassment. "Of course. I'm sorry to have interrupted, and it was good to see you again."

Flustered and hurt by his attitude too many times in the space of a couple hours, Lyra departed as fast as she could. Maggie noticed her distress immediately and rushed to her side with their purses.

"Are you okay?"

"I need to leave—now." Lyra strode to the door and waited while Maggie went to the front desk to pay.

Colin politely refused to accept the company business card Maggie handed him. "The meal is paid for, Ms. St. Claire."

She froze for a second. "I'd rather pay for my own food."

He grimaced. "Do you want to be the one to tell Chef Hunter?"

"No!" Lyra took a deep breath. Colin had been so attentive and looked genuinely sorry. He didn't deserve to be raked over the coals for this, and with no desire to argue with Kaden, it meant swallowing her pride about receiving the free meals.

"Don't trouble him, but please thank him very much, and tell him again that the food was wonderful."

With a glance at the kitchen doors, Colin helped them into their coats. "It means a great deal to him that you came here and tried his dishes, even if he won't tell you that. Have a good evening. I hope to see you back sometime."

His apologetic manner and words confused her further, and once they walked out into the cool evening, Lyra stalled at the curb, reliving each moment.

Maggie tucked her own scarf tighter and waited beside her. "What just happened?" she asked finally.

Lyra swallowed hard. "He's annoyed that I left him behind and didn't contact him, even though I tried to explain what it was like for me. We trained together side by side for three years and were such good friends. I can honestly say I don't remember him ever being truly annoyed with me over anything."

Maggie screwed up her nose. "He might be a hunk, but if he can't see that you care, then you shouldn't fret over him. Trust me, it's a waste of time and feelings."

Lyra would normally agree, but she was still trying to digest the way Kaden had treated her. Maybe she deserved his disdain and disappointment for not being available the way a good friend should be. With her agent managing her work schedule, there simply wasn't time to chase him down. She'd called, texted, and left messages that first year; then, after some time when she still couldn't reach him, she assumed he didn't want to keep in contact.

Still, it wasn't Kaden's way to be rude or uncharitable, and it seemed important to explain this to Maggie.

"Kaden always encouraged me whenever I wanted to try something new and made the failures matter less. Something else must have happened to make him react this way."

Her mind spiraled, thinking back to that blurry part of life. She'd barely had time to tell her mom and pack before being whisked away. It was the job of a lifetime, and she couldn't turn it down. She'd said her goodbyes, and Kaden seemed happy for her, but did he actually believe she should have stayed?

Maggie tucked her arm in Lyra's, and they began to walk. "Okay, so he's worth a little effort. He said he tried to contact you. Several times."

Lyra shrugged. "Maybe he tried, but after the first month or so, I only heard from him once or twice in that first year. This was way before you started working for me, and my agent handled all my calls. In the beginning, Symon kept my schedule and made sure I wasn't distracted by anyone. Unfortunately, it meant Mom and my friends were also kept at bay. I explained all that, and they seemed okay about it." She stopped in the middle of the path. "Now that I think about it, I called Kaden about that, but I never spoke to him. I guess a part of me thought he would understand."

Maggie frowned. "That's not the impression I got. It really sounded like he'd tried hard that first year. Unless his calls didn't reach you?"

They stared at each other.

Something about that time nagged at her. "He had my personal number, but then I lost my phone. When I got the new one, Symon set it up for me. He also promised to contact Kaden when he saw how upset I was."

"Doesn't that make you suspicious?"

Lyra nodded. "Symon is a control freak, but he knew how I felt about the isolation. Plus, no matter how guilty I feel about not making more of an effort to reach him, Kaden did the same thing."

Maggie shrugged. "Yet he won't take any responsibility for his part."

They continued on their walk back to the hotel with Lyra lost in her thoughts. Cinnamon ran to her as soon as they entered the apartment. Lyra dropped to her knees to embrace her best friend. It had once been Kaden, but when those bonds were severed, Lyra needed someone to lavish her affection on, and the dog shelter proved the perfect place to look. Much to her agent's annoyance.

For perhaps the first time, she'd put her foot down. When she refused to return the pup from an abandoned litter, Symon opted to make Cinnamon famous too. This worked out perfectly once Symon began leasing a plane, because then she could take the beagle almost anywhere.

Maggie went to her room to call her family, and Lyra initially thought she would do the same, but instead of her mom, she needed to talk to Symon. With the urge to see his face when she questioned him, she turned on her laptop and used a video app instead of just a phone call.

He appeared instantly and Cinnamon growled. For a reason known only to the beagle, Symon had never been her favorite person.

"Lyra, darling, I've missed you. Is everything all right?"

She smiled. He was always effusive, and the intimacy of his endearments had long since ceased to bother her. Despite rubbing people the wrong way, he did work hard for her. Although lately he'd been absent more than usual, giving Maggie more of his responsibilities. Fortunately, her assistant took to the heavier workload like a duck to water, and Lyra preferred her company. "The show went well, but that's not why I called. I need to ask you a question."

He leaned back against the white couch in his penthouse apartment in LA. "Shoot."

"When I first went to LA for the show, and you became my agent—"

"The best moment of my life," he interrupted with a self-satisfied smile.

She nodded. "Thank you. Anyway, I had a good friend try to contact me back then."

Symon snorted. "There were plenty of hangers-on in the beginning. I can't begin to tell you how many."

Her smile cracked. "I'm talking about my best friend, Kaden Hunter. Does the name ring any bells?"

He picked a piece of lint off his suit trousers. "The name does sound familiar. Why?"

"I just bumped into him at his restaurant, and he says he tried for a year to reach me—and never could after the first few times."

Symon lifted his hands in the air. "We did change your phone number at least twice, to stop all the unnecessary calls you were bombarded with. I recall you lost your phone once too."

"That's right, and you said you would send my new number to the list I gave you and keep calling Kaden for me."

A telling pause followed, and she leaned forward to where the laptop was propped against her bag on the table. Her stomach churned. "Is that what happened, Symon?"

He clasped his hands behind his head with a false casualness. "I did send the number to your mom and a few friends."

She kept her voice neutral. "Why would you leave anyone off, and Kaden in particular?"

He gave a wry smile. "I told you from the start that it's a good look for you to be single. Seeing you involved in any romantic entanglement, even one that's only perceived to be so, could have harmed your ratings."

As he went off on his "what's best for your career is the only important thing" spiel, Lyra clenched her teeth. It had gotten old a long time ago. He might have been good at his job, but he crossed the line too often, and this was one major step too far.

"How dare you decide something like that. You had no right!" Her voice rose above his, and Cinnamon growled again.

He sat up straighter but, to her frustration, didn't back down.

"Well, that's easy to say now that you're famous. Back then I was looking out for your fledgling career, and I believe it's paid dividends. Wouldn't you agree?"

Instead of arguing, Lyra picked up Cinnamon, rubbing her face in the softness of her fur, a way of calming herself that usually worked better than it did now. She would always acknowledge Symon's role in her career successes, but she was over his interference in every aspect of her life. "You did do a good job, but that doesn't excuse the decisions you made like this one. I'm tired. We can talk more tomorrow."

He leaned closer. "Yes, it sounds like you need a good rest, and I hope to see you when you get back to town."

The plaintiveness was not attractive, and she couldn't bring herself to promise him any such thing. "Good night, Symon."

She closed the app and let out a breath. It was obvious now that Kaden wasn't to blame. She'd bet every cupcake she made that Symon never once called Kaden.

Clipping on Cinnamon's leash, she called out to Maggie that she was taking the beagle for a quick walk.

Donning her recently discarded coat and scarf, they did a few laps of the small park opposite the hotel. Cinnamon hugged her ankles so closely that Lyra almost tripped several times. The beagle's uncanny knack of sensing Lyra's mood warmed her a little. Large caramel eyes kept gazing upward, and Lyra crouched to cuddle the soft warmth and have kisses rain upon her face.

With no clear idea how to fix things with Kaden, she simply knew she had to try. Otherwise, she would continue to feel as though she'd failed him. Busy or not, Lyra should have dug deeper into why she hadn't heard from her friend. Tomorrow she would find a way to speak to Kaden.

A shadow flitted between the trees ahead, and Cinnamon barked. Lyra looked around them as she spoke softly. "What is it, Cin?"

The beagle whined, tugging at the lead. They'd walked quite a way into the park, and she could no longer see the street, which was careless so late at night after what had happened.

"Let's go home," she urged.

The beagle was happy to comply, although she looked back over her shoulder several times as they walked briskly back to the street.

## 8

___

It was another brilliant day, which didn't mean Lyra could afford to walk around without the coat or the cap she wore low over her forehead, her red hair in a ponytail tucked beneath it. Any die-hard fans, knowing she was in town, might still notice her, but if she dressed this way, the chances were kept to a minimum.

All night she'd tossed and turned thinking about Kaden, then woke with a sense of purpose. Although it was hours before lunch service, as a chef, Lyra knew the day began hours earlier. That meant there was every chance that Kaden was already at Phoenix.

Opting to go alone instead of asking Maggie to accompany her made sense. Kaden was angry, and angry people usually said terrible things. The last thing Lyra wanted was Maggie giving him a piece of her mind because she thought she was protecting Lyra.

Not that there was any guarantee they could have a discussion alone. That definitely bothered her. Years in the spotlight taught her that people loved drama. The press were forever looking for ways to find dirt on anyone with Lyra's status. So far, she'd come off okay, though it was never assured. It only took one person to appreciate that they could sell a snippet, and a secret could hit the headlines without warning.

She'd known chefs who'd lost their positions and occasionally their restaurants when something surfaced that painted them in a bad light. Even if it was a lie. With that weighing on her, Lyra had to take this chance to make things right between her and Kaden.

How could she make him see that throwing their friendship away hurt them both?

Not bothering with the front entrance, which would probably be locked until nearer opening time, she went to the back door. It stood open with only a screen in place to keep out flying insects. Inside, the hustle and bustle of a well-organized kitchen created a pang of longing. It was all very well traveling for different causes or shows, but she badly missed being in a kitchen.

She took in a calming breath and knocked on the frame. Several pairs of eyes turned her way, and when Lyra unwrapped her scarf, a young woman dropped the pile of metal trays she was carrying. They clanged loudly, drawing the remaining staff's attention. A man peeling potatoes stared and rubbed his eyes. When she didn't disappear, he stared some more.

"What's going on in here?" Kaden came out of a room to the side of the door. "We've got a wedding party coming in tonight, and standing around isn't going to get them fed."

He sounded puzzled rather than annoyed, and she took that as a good sign.

"It-it-it's Lyra St. Claire." The young woman pointed.

Kaden followed the finger, his face reflecting several emotions. As best she could tell from outside the screen door, happiness wasn't one of them.

BEAGLES LOVE CUPCAKE CRIMES

"Did you leave something behind?" He crossed the room and unlocked the door.

"More like someone," she croaked.

He frowned. "Are you ill?"

She shook her head. "I need to talk to you, if you have a minute."

"I don't have half a minute."

"Twenty seconds?" she pressed.

His staff were glued to the exchange, and, suddenly aware of their audience, Kaden released a heavy sigh. "You'd better come through to my office."

Lyra lifted the lead she held. "Do you mind if I bring Cinnamon?"

Kaden looked down to her beagle. The surprise slipped into a smile. "You always wanted a dog, and a beagle in particular," he said, giving Cinnamon a good scratch behind her ears.

Cinnamon rolled onto her back, and the other staff cooed over Kaden's shoulder as she made little snorts of pleasure when he continued the treatment on her stomach. One back leg convulsed over and over with every scratch.

Lyra felt a rush of affection for them both. Cinnamon allowing anyone other than Lyra and Maggie to pet her anywhere other than her head or back was a rare sight. Kaden being the one to have the privilege of making Cinnamon so happy was so sweet. That and the fact that he'd remembered her wanting a beagle.

He casually took the lead from her hand and picked up Cinnamon. "Come on through. As long as we have no inspectors drop by, she'll be fine in my office."

Cinnamon didn't seem to have any misgivings, so Lyra followed, unbuttoning her coat along the way and smiling at the staff.

Kaden put Cinnamon on the floor and took Lyra's coat,

hanging it on a rack behind the door, which he closed. Then he pulled out a chair for her before sitting behind the desk, still with Cinnamon's lead in his hand. Her dog sat at his feet, staring at him adoringly.

"She's very cute." Kaden lifted Cinnamon onto his lap, which was also something the beagle didn't often permit.

"She is," Lyra agreed. "And she seems to like you."

"So, what brought you back?" he asked.

Lyra clasped her hands together on her plum-colored dress. "My agent's confession."

His hand stilled in Cinnamon's short coat. "Pardon me?"

Their eyes locked, and Lyra gulped.

"I did call you many times when I first left, and you called me too, but then the calls stopped. I made excuses at first, like the time difference, exams, and the pressure of work. But now I know there was another factor. Symon Reeves, my agent, made sure your calls never reached me. I'd lost my phone, and I never checked when he set up my new one that your number was correct." She handed him her phone, and he checked the number under his name.

"That's not mine."

"I guessed as much. I don't remember anyone's number except mine, do you?"

He shook his head. "Still…."

"I know. I could have called someone else to check. It simply never occurred to me. Symon decided, without asking what I thought, that you would negatively affect my career. I simply thought you were busy like I was. I get that it's not a good enough excuse, but eventually I assumed you'd moved on with new, more available friends."

Kaden looked away; his fingers combed Cinnamon's fur just the way Lyra's did when deep in thought.

"That's not how friendship works." Though he didn't look

up, his voice was softer, giving her hope. "When I commit to someone, I don't give up on them."

"Seems to me that you did exactly that," she said regretfully.

Now he did look at her. "No, that was different. Your star was shining bright after just a few months. I figured you had no time for a lesser wannabe."

Lyra grimaced. "You know me better than that. At least, you used to."

He had the decency to look shamefaced. "Even if I accept that your agent engineered what happened, we're both different now. You don't even live here anymore."

She smiled gently. "Do we really need to be in the same city to be friends?"

His hand stilled, and Cinnamon wriggled underneath his touch to encourage him to continue.

"What kind of friends?"

"Ones who won't let others interfere ever again. I really missed you, Kaden." The words poured from her heart with the hope that he wouldn't reject her a second time.

"I missed you too, but I bet you have plenty of people to keep you company."

Lyra's courage almost failed her. She leaned forward in earnest, not wanting to waste her one chance to make things right between them. "Sure, I have dozens of people hanging around me. People more interested in my fame than me. Do you crave those kinds of people in your life? The ones who always say yes? Or, just as frequently, the 'no' people. Because I don't. I want friends who know me and speak to me honestly about my ideas and the mundane things in life as well as celebrating the highs and dealing with the lows. You were that person for me. I want you to be again."

He looked up and frowned. "I don't know if we can ever go back. I hear it's not so easy."

"Can we at least try?" Lyra wouldn't beg, but she wasn't ready to give up.

Cinnamon tilted her head, then stood on Kaden's lap and licked his chin. Caramel eyes pleaded with him.

"Did you train your dog to do that?" he accused her with a tender smile as he hugged Cinnamon closer.

Lyra laughed, a little choked up. "Not at all. Cinnamon seems to know when people are upset, and she wants to help. It's one of the many things I love about her."

Kaden scratched Cinnamon between the ears while he looked at Lyra with an expression she couldn't decide was good or bad.

"When are you going back to LA?" he asked.

"Tonight."

He steepled his fingers, and his eyes narrowed a little. "I suppose you're busy until then?"

"I'm packed and free until my driver picks Maggie, Cinnamon, and me up. Why?"

He leaned back, Cinnamon sprawling across his knees.

"I'm down one chef, and we have the place booked for a wedding party."

Lyra hadn't seen that coming, and her fingertips tingled with the idea of cooking with him once more. "You're really asking me to cook for you?"

"Do you still know how?" he challenged, eyes twinkling.

She was tempted to poke out her tongue like she would have once upon a time. "Now you're being rude, and I do believe you're testing me."

He gave a small chuckle. "Perhaps I'm testing how far a friendship will go."

"Okay." Lyra relaxed into the chair, delighted by the shock on his face.

Kaden sat bolt upright and Cinnamon scrambled up

Kaden's body so as not to fall. He managed to grab hold of her at the last moment.

"Pardon?"

She shrugged. "I'll cook for you. Show me where my station is, and I'm all yours."

"In that?" Kaden nodded at the fitted dress she wore.

"It'll be a waste of time to go back to the hotel. Although, I could get Maggie to pop down here with a change of clothes and some shoes that won't kill me to walk a few hours in."

She pulled out her phone, calling Maggie as she spoke. Kaden grinned as if he'd won a prize, then stood and placed Cinnamon carefully on his seat.

"Here you go, sweetie. You're in charge while your mom and I go have some fun."

Cinnamon barked, did a 360-degree turn, then curled up on the chair. She was going to be just fine here until Maggie could take her back to the hotel.

Call made, Kaden handed her an apron. "It might help for now."

"Thanks, Chef," she said cheekily as they walked back into the kitchen. Her heart fluttered the way it did before the camera lights turned green, or before she walked out on stage. Yet it wasn't the thought of cooking with other people or cooking well. It was that she was cooking with Kaden like they used to. Her biggest hope was that he really could forgive her and that this wasn't simply about needing another pair of hands.

When they saw her, the staff stopped once more.

"Okay, take a good look at the star in our midst, then get back to work. Chef St. Claire is helping us out today. If you need advice, ask, but don't gawk or annoy her. Understood?"

"Yes, Chef!" they chorused, still staring.

Lyra smiled at them. "Let's get this show cooking." It was her catchphrase on *A Lesson with Lyra*, and they laughed delightedly, except for a slim woman who stood at the back of the room. She didn't seem happy at all, but perhaps she was nervous. Sometimes having someone famous around made others feel uneasy at being judged or doing something wrong.

Lyra turned back to Kaden. "May I see the menu?"

A stocky man had come from the other side of the room and stood beside Kaden.

"I'm Michel Fortneau. It's a great pleasure to meet you in person and to work with you. We're all very grateful for your help." He handed her a card with every dish listed. "Come, see how we make these."

Kaden nodded. "I'll catch up with you soon."

Once she'd washed her hands, Michel took her to the stations so she could see what each of them was working on and get an idea on where she could fit in. It was good to learn the staff's names, and the Frenchman revealed his pride at working here, the food they made, and his team.

"This is Rita Lowe. She's been with us since we opened."

"Hi, Rita. You're in charge of the vegetables, I see."

The woman looked down at her station. "I guess you have people to do the prep for you on your shows."

"Most of the time, but I am hands-on as much as possible."

Rita nodded. "Adam Lancaster sure was lucky to win that competition."

"He worked very hard to get there. Maybe you could enter next year?"

"Me?"

"Why not? Working here, I'm sure you're picking up lots of tips and experience. Take my word for it, you never know when your lucky break will come, so you do need to put yourself out there."

This was her thing. Making people feel at ease while

enjoying the art of cooking. It meant tamping down any imposter syndrome she might be clinging to and living in the moment. The end result was the goal, and you got there faster if everyone pulled together.

At least that was the theory. Rita didn't appear to appreciate her humor or encouragement, so Lyra moved on.

## 9

---

Side by side, Kaden and Lyra worked as if the years had rolled away and they were in the training kitchen not more than a couple miles from here. Except now they were more accomplished and understood better what worked and what didn't. Lyra took notice of everyone, and every dish, as did Kaden. This way they knew before it went out the door that each plate would be perfect.

Always good, now he was an excellent chef, and his staff were devoted to him. No task appeared to be too small or too daunting for any of them, especially the woman who stayed well away from Lyra but paid great attention to detail. When she wasn't watching Kaden. *Are they an item?* Well, it was none of her business if they were, and he deserved to be happy. He certainly looked like he was.

Kaden's restaurant had all the ingredients necessary to be considered great. She recognized it immediately, because she not only saw it but also felt it. Phoenix had the recipe right just like La Joliesse, and the fact that they had both achieved their dreams made her smile.

Colin arrived while they were preparing for service and

came straight to Lyra's station, beaming at her. "I heard you were assisting today, but I couldn't quite believe it."

"I could hardly leave a friend in the lurch." She nodded at Kaden.

"Lucky for us." Kaden grinned. "You're early, Colin."

"I knew we were short-staffed, so I thought I could help somehow."

Kaden snorted. "Not just to watch Lyra St. Claire in action?"

"That's a bonus for sure." Colin chuckled.

"It looks great out there." Kaden nodded toward the restaurant. "You must have worked late last night."

"Not just me. Angie was a big help. Such an important wedding has the potential to lead to many more. We all want that, so it has to be perfect." Colin checked his watch. "By my calculations, the first guests will be arriving in one hour."

"We're mostly cleaning up now. The mains are still cooking, but all the desserts are made, and the entrees are ready for plating." Kaden put his arm on Colin's shoulder. "I'm sure it's perfect, but I'd like to give the restaurant layout a final inspection."

"I wouldn't have it any other way. Lyra, would you like to come?" Colin asked hopefully.

"Yes, please." She was already washing her hands again.

The room was resplendent in pink and purple. Purple for the chair covers, tablecloths in pink, and the centerpieces a mixture of Oregon iris and peace tea roses.

"You already put the flowers out," Kaden mused. "You must have arrived ages ago."

Colin shook his head. "I can't take the credit. Apparently Lyra's assistant positioned them on the tables and tweaked each one."

"Is she here? They look perfect, and I'd like to thank her."

Lyra grinned. "You were busy when Maggie came by to

pick up Cinnamon. She studied interior designing, adores weddings, and couldn't resist helping before she left. I'll let her know you approve."

He grinned back. "Now that everything is in order, I'll get changed, then open the doors. Will you put the place cards out, please, Colin?"

"I'll help him with that," Lyra offered, not yet ready to leave. She hadn't realized just how much she'd missed him until today.

"You don't have to. I'm sure you want to get back to the hotel and get ready for your flight."

She shook her head. "No way. I've worked too hard to miss seeing the wedding party arrive. Besides, I already called my pilot to arrange a later departure time."

Kaden snorted. "You have your own pilot?"

A little embarrassed, Lyra shrugged. "I travel a lot, so I lease a plane. It's necessary so I can bring Cinnamon with me."

With an amused look, Kaden spread his arms. "In that case, feel free. Just having you here is a bonus, so we'll take all the time you choose to give us."

With a squeeze of her shoulders, he left Colin and Lyra to lay out the cards. The two of them worked fast. Soon they were done, and for the final touch, Colin erected a stand with table assignments on a large board at the entrance.

"Thank you for your help," Colin said as they returned to the kitchen. "It's always a relief to have things finished when we get these important clients."

"My pleasure. It's the mayor's daughter's wedding, isn't it?"

"That's right, Antonia Clements. It's been hush-hush until recently, but you know how hard it is to keep a secret from the media."

"Almost impossible," Lyra agreed. "I met the mayor and

his wife yesterday at the cooking competition. They're a lovely couple, and I don't imagine this will be a small reception."

Colin grimaced. "The wedding was held at St. Bart's, and pretty much everyone they knew was invited. As you can imagine, that was half the town, and they were lined up thirty deep outside the church. We've utilized every conceivable space, but they still had to cull the guest list to make it work."

"Wow. I bet there are some people put out about not making the reception list."

Colin nodded. "It appears so. Kaden suggested they put up a tent outside the church for everyone to offer congratulations, and we provided the refreshments. That extra work and a person down is why we were so far behind this morning, so thank goodness you were willing to help. The reception is supposed to be just family and close friends. Plus one or two celebrities." He waggled his eyebrows at her.

She laughed, impressed with Kaden's ambition and his team. It was no wonder the restaurant was doing so well. "It's a clever idea to run the whole thing foodwise, even if it is at two places. I have a big wedding myself coming up that I'm catering at another venue because the guest list is massive, which has its own logistical issues, but if I do get an event like the mayor and his family, thanks to Kaden, it's good to know it can be done another way."

Colin smiled. "Kaden will be pleased he had an idea you might use."

A burning question burst out of her like a recipe that had percolated far too long. "How's he been?" She genuinely wanted to know if his life was as good as it looked.

"He's great. Phoenix makes Kaden happy. Then again, I don't know how he was before," he said wryly.

"Of course. I don't mean to pry. I can appreciate how hard

he must have worked to get where he is. It can't have been easy."

"It wasn't." Colin shrugged. "Kaden's a proud man, and deservedly so. Without a backer, he made Phoenix what she is through determination and a ton of hard work. He can tell you that story, but the restaurant is doing far better than either of us predicted. Now I must get changed."

Colin's abrupt departure must have been due to them discussing Kaden so openly. His loyalty reminded her of George, the maître d' at La Joliesse, and she was glad he had people around him like that.

Lyra went back to Kaden's office to change back into her original outfit. A knock at the door came just as she was running a brush through her thick hair.

"Come in," she called, smoothing down her dress.

Kaden leaned against the doorframe. "That dress really suits you and fits in well with the wedding decor."

She laughed. "It's like I planned it."

He tilted his head. "Did you?"

Her mouth dropped open for a second. He wasn't asking about the dress. "How on earth could I have done that?"

"Maybe someone told you I'd be short-staffed today?" he suggested.

"I knew nothing about this wedding or your staffing issues," Lyra ground out. "I simply wanted to help."

His mouth twitched. "All right, don't get hot under the collar. I believe you."

She flicked a towel at him. "You were teasing?"

"You used to get when I was."

He was grinning, and she realized the mood was one she recognized. One she'd loved and missed nearly as much as she missed him.

"It's a darn shame I don't have a cake in my hand," she threatened.

He raised an eyebrow. "I'd have thought at our age we'd gone past that stage."

She raised an eyebrow. "Never assume something like that."

The grin widened, and another jolt of recognition hit her. This really was the old Kaden. The one who'd taught her to trust her instincts. The one who'd been her champion when she pulled something off that no one else did. The one who said, *"Take the job with the TV show. You're a natural. You got this."*

He roared with laughter. "I guess I'd better not if I want to keep you as a friend."

"Good friend," she added, needing to clarify it and hoping he felt that way too.

The waitress from the night before poked her head around the door, giving Lyra a pink-cheeked smile before addressing her.

"Colin says to tell you that the wedding party's arriving."

Used to fans, Lyra smiled back in the friendly way she'd branded as her own. "Wonderful. Where can I watch from?"

Kaden pointed. "There's a small mezzanine floor, just up those stairs."

"I didn't notice them. What a cool idea." She put her foot on the bottom step. "What's your waitress's name?"

He gave her a curious look. "Angela Leigh. We call her Angie. As for the stairs and the mezzanine, I got them put in when I first bought the place and was refurbishing the whole inside. The ceiling space is so large, it seemed a shame to waste it, and I thought it would be handy to get a good perspective of the whole operation from time to time. It can also double as storage. Plus I've been known to have a nap on the couch over there when we've had a busy night."

Lyra laughed as she reached the top of the narrow staircase and saw where he was pointing. The couch tucked under an eave looked very comfortable indeed.

Proud of his achievement and clear vision, Lyra stood beside him to look out over the glass balustrade while Kaden pointed out various aspects of the setup for the wedding.

"I love the concept of seeing the layout from another angle and having a place to nap or to just get off your feet for a bit. Plus, you could always put more tables up here if you needed to."

"I've thought of it, but I think the number of tables we have is more than enough for the kitchen to cope with."

"Good point. There's no point in making things harder. What's that for?" Lyra pointed to where a camera sat on an almost hidden shelf.

Kaden pulled it down. "I've never seen this before. It's some kind of fancy recorder. He hasn't mentioned it, but maybe Colin's looking at upgrading our security."

Just then the guests began to come through the open main doors, and the place filled up quickly. Rose petals, taken from small paper bags handed to the guests prior to the bridal party arriving, were thrown on the couple as they walked up the middle of the room to the bridal table. The bride squealed but looked delighted with the attention, while the groom wore an expression of tolerant amusement.

They were a cute couple, and she imagined the ceremony would have been magnificent. She did love a good wedding and hoped one day she might enjoy a day like this. Unfortunately, she hadn't met anyone she could even consider dating, let alone anything more romantic.

Naturally, she blamed Kaden. He was the standard that she measured men by and, funnily, still had, even when they were estranged.

"They look happy," he whispered in her ear.

His breath tickled her neck, and she laughed. "Stunning as well."

The wedding dress was simply gorgeous. Lyra wondered if it was made by a woman she'd met before—a fashionista for the curvier woman like herself and the gorgeous woman below her.

It was exceptionally hard to find clothes that not only fit but also encompassed her style. The so-called boutiques with this in mind didn't come close to expectations, and picking up something like the dress she wore today was rare. Maybe if she hung around for a while, she might have a chance to ask the bride who made it.

That thought disappeared when she saw the parents of the bride and the groom. The mayor and his wife were comfortable with the noise, while the other couple appeared hesitant and then relieved to get away from the crowd and take their seats.

She had been like that couple before her career flourished. It took a great deal of time and practice to be okay with being the center of attention.

The emcee began his speech, and Lyra appreciated that time alone with the bride to discuss her dress was probably never going to happen. She looked at her watch. If everything went to plan, she could stay for the main course, but then she needed to go. Her pilot had already delayed the flight a few hours so she could be here, and he had family to get home to. To save more time, Maggie would come to Phoenix with the bags and Cinnamon so they could leave from here.

Lyra gazed around the room and noticed the kitchen door was half open. Rita stood there, but her attention was on the mezzanine and not the guests. Eyes flashing, she glared at Lyra.

"It's a good start, and it looks like they're ready for the

first course" Kaden was saying. Then he frowned when he saw where she was looking. "What the heck is she doing there?"

Michel arrived at the kitchen door, and whatever he said to the young chef made her cheeks red. She slipped away into the kitchen with one last glance at the mezzanine.

"What's she done wrong?" Lyra asked.

"Rita's a hard worker, but she always thinks she knows best. I want to promote her, but she interferes with everyone else's work and never apologizes. I have no time for that kind of arrogance." Kaden shook his head. "Never mind. Michel will get her under control, and we have the best view in the house."

Lyra looked over the balcony at the guests. It was definitely a lively and beautiful group of people.

And clearly, Rita was not Kaden's girlfriend.

## 10

As the first course came out, Kaden nodded in satisfaction. "I can't begin to thank you for today and tonight."

Lyra grinned. "Give it a try."

He nudged her gently with his shoulder. "Having you lend a hand definitely made all the difference to the success of this wedding. One of the staff let it slip that you're here, and the guests are feeling pretty special right now."

Lyra frowned. "That's not fair. I helped cook, but the menu's yours."

He shook his head. "You know how a celebrity in the room trumps even the best food."

She did know it. She was hounded almost every day and in the weirdest places without lifting a spoon or an ingredient. Even the bathroom wasn't a space too intimate to intrude on.

Lyra sighed. "Does it bother you? I can go down there and explain to everyone."

He shook his head. "This is one night out of a year, and not the norm. Besides, having the famous Lyra St. Claire cooking at Phoenix will undoubtedly encourage other diners or bookings like this. Word of mouth and the hope it might be repeated shouldn't be underestimated. You and I know, which is all that matters."

She clasped his hand, which was rough in comparison to hers and showed how much work he did in the kitchen. "Really? Are you sure?"

Looking down, he put her hand to his lips. "Thanks for the offer, but tonight I really am happy with everything."

"I should at least speak to the mayor." She made to walk past him, but he held onto her hand.

"Honestly, it's not necessary. Colin will set him straight."

"Did you ask him to do that?"

"I didn't have to. Colin has an uncanny way of making things right. Even with the hardest-nosed paparazzi in attendance."

Lyra didn't know Colin but understood that Kaden's success was due in part to having the man by his side no matter what Colin said about Kaden doing it alone. Sharing a passion and the drive to get Phoenix to this stage had likely cemented the close bond they appeared to have.

She scanned the guests again. "I didn't notice any paparazzi on the guest list."

He snorted. "You've been away too long and, dare I say, too protected to pick them out."

Lyra heard censure in his voice, which annoyed her. "You mean because of my agent?"

"Symon Reeves has a reputation for being the trickiest in the business."

She could hardly deny it but couldn't bring herself to agree. "I'm not sure if that's the best recommendation for what he does."

"Years ago, maybe not, but everyone knows he's picked up

a few clients because of his involvement with you, not because he's the best or pleasant to work with."

Kaden had clearly formed an opinion of the agent that wasn't favorable, and he was entitled to feel strongly about what Symon had done to them. Interestingly, by the sound of it, Kaden might also know more about Symon's dealings than she did.

"Has he really picked up more clients because of me?"

Kaden raised an eyebrow. "Surely you didn't think you were his only one. After four years of working with him, you can't be that naïve."

Lyra pushed her hair back from her shoulders irritably. "Of course not. He has another couple of people he works for, but we don't discuss who else he represents. Since he's not exclusive to me, it's not my business to ask."

She watched him wrestle with his thoughts. Then he sighed as if he couldn't contain them.

"Wise move on his part not telling you who they are when some of them are less savory than your beacon of niceness."

She grimaced. "Bleh. You make me sound like bottled water—bland and easy to purchase."

"Poor little rich girl," he teased.

She wanted honesty. Craved it. Therefore, how could she stay angry with him? "Only one of those titles fits."

He raised an eyebrow. "I guess you're not a girl anymore."

She batted him on the arm, relieved at the lighter banter. He'd always told her the truth, and right then Lyra knew she needed to have him around again and would do whatever was necessary to make that happen.

"I'll be sorry to see you go," Kaden blurted as if he'd read her mind.

"It's been so much fun. You have an awesome team, and you should be proud of Phoenix. I love her."

He grinned. "I'm glad you do, and I am proud of her. Prouder than anything I've ever done in my life."

She tilted her head. "What about convincing me to go to LA?"

"You would have done that without me."

Lyra frowned. "You know that's not true. You said all the right things. You made me believe I could do it."

He stared into her eyes, and she saw a sadness there. "Well, I wasn't wrong, was I?"

"As far as I know—" She gulped. "—the only time you've ever been truly wrong was believing I could possibly forget you."

He pushed back a strand of her hair, his fingers touching her cheek. "Let's agree to disagree on that."

In a moment of madness, Lyra hugged him. "Whatever you say, Chef. As long as you're talking to me, I'll let you think you're right about anything."

Colin gave a polite cough from the stairs. "Could you spare a minute to accept thanks from the mayor and his family?"

Kaden's arms dropped. "Of course. Lyra, will you come?"

"Are you sure you want me there?" She tried to make it sound teasing, but she truly didn't want her celebrity status to outshine him on this special day.

He winked. "Like I said, it couldn't hurt business."

She screwed up her nose. "As long as I'm good for something."

They descended to the main floor and followed Colin over to the bridal table. The mayor leaped from his seat and pumped Kaden's hand.

"Well done, young man. I had no idea you were friends with Lyra and that she was helping tonight. The two of you carried this off beautifully, and my daughter is delighted with everything."

The bride also got to her feet to hug Kaden. "The place is amazing. I knew you'd do it."

"Thanks, Antonia." He kissed her cheek. "You deserve all of this."

Lyra watched the interchange with interest, and then Kaden made the introductions.

"Lyra St. Claire, this is Antonia Clements and her parents, Mayor Clements and Mrs. Clements, whom you've already met."

They shook hands.

"Actually, it's Clements-Taylor now," the bride corrected him, smiling serenely at her new groom, who was more reticent, although he did stand and shake their hands.

"Would it be okay to have a photo with both of you?" the mayor asked. "For Antonia."

"I'm afraid Lyra is about to leave," Kaden apologized. "She has a plane to catch and was only helping out as a favor."

"I have time for a few photos," Lyra interrupted.

The bride beamed, and her bridesmaid, who gaped at Lyra, was dispatched to fetch the photographer.

A few turned out to be dozens. Finally, Lyra, her cheeks stiffening from smiling so much, excused herself to heartfelt thanks.

Kaden escorted her to his office. He closed the door, and they faced each other, grinning for a minute or two. When he opened his arms, she went without hesitation. Time shifted, and they were once more the younger versions of themselves enjoying a shared success. A secret moment of pure pleasure and pride, and now it had to end.

"My car will be waiting outside. Thanks for a fun day," Lyra said into his chest.

He kissed the top of her head and let her go. "Fun but exhausting."

She collected her coat and bag. "A good exhaustion, and one I won't forget in a hurry."

"Me either. I'm so glad you came by." He coughed. "There's just the little matter of who's going to call whom?"

She pulled a card from her bag and tucked it into his shirt pocket. "I mean what I say about staying in touch. I will call you, but now that you have my private number, neither of us has an excuse."

He hugged her again, only harder. Was he thinking about the whole "out of sight, out of mind" scenario as well? She was at a loss to find more words needed to convince him to trust her.

Finally, Kaden gently pushed her away. "In that case, get going so you can call me."

He walked her to the car, and Dan jumped out to open the door for her. There was no point in dragging this out any longer, but she couldn't resist another brief hug before climbing in.

A camera flashed from somewhere in the dark, but she didn't care. Then the car pulled away, and just like that, the best day she'd had in a while was over.

Cinnamon clambered onto her lap and nuzzled Lyra's cheek. Burying her face in the warm neck she relived several moments. Maggie would be waiting for a rehash of the evening, but kindly stayed quiet, giving Lyra time to think how she could make a relationship with Kaden work from so far away and not mess things up again.

## 11

The plane hit the tarmac with a shudder, and Lyra flinched. Private jet or not, flying would never be her preferred mode of transportation, despite it being less than two and a half hours from Portland to Los Angeles.

"Are you okay?" Maggie touched Lyra's white-knuckled grasp on the armrest.

Lyra sighed wearily. "I will be once my feet touch the ground."

"It's a shame you can't enjoy all this." Maggie waved at the cabin. "I wonder if you'll ever get used to it."

Her assistant's concern was touching. When Lyra first started out in this business and just had the show, there was little travel, which suited her fine. But once the books began to come out and she needed to cross the country for celebrity spots on other shows and competitions she judged, things changed dramatically.

Eventually, leasing a plane became necessary. It gave her more time on the ground and alleviated situations at airports where she would normally be subjected to crowds and fans who often acted like her personal space wasn't anything worth worrying about.

Even that positive side to flying, including an amazing find in her pilot, didn't negate the anxiousness or worry over every bump. "There's always hope that one day I will." Lyra sighed again.

Cinnamon got to her feet in the next seat, stretched, then gave Lyra's hand a lick. Only one of them hated flying. The ultimate traveler, Cinnamon didn't worry about cars or planes, using them as a means to catch up on naps. If only Lyra could do the same.

Undoing both of their seat belts, Cinnamon's designed especially for her, Lyra bundled the beagle into her arms. She was another major factor in leasing a plane. Now they could go wherever they wished and not worry about crates or cages. Having her sweet pet by her side almost twenty-four-seven was worth the expense. Cinnamon also did wonders to keep Lyra calm enough to travel. Once she'd used pills to help the anxiety; now she simply wrapped her fingers in the short fur, felt the strong heartbeat beneath, and looked into those warm brown eyes for reassurance.

The main door was opened by the hostess, and the pilot, Jim Easton, came through from the cockpit.

"Thanks for the good flight, Jim."

Knowing how bad she was at this, he smiled warmly. "I managed to get up out of any turbulence without any hassle from aviation."

"You know how much I appreciate that." Always happier once they landed, she found it an effort not to hug the poor man.

Jim nodded. "No problem. I haven't gotten any further bookings from Symon, so I guess you're staying put for a bit?"

"As far as I know, I'm here for the next month. Lucky for

me, Symon mixed up a couple dates." She winked. "And I hear you have some well-deserved time off planned anyway. Enjoy the break with your family."

"I will." He frowned. "Although, Disneyland is on the wish list for the kids, and I hate rides."

Lyra snorted. "That seems rather odd when you bounce around the skies as often as you do."

"Bounce? I think you have me confused with Snoopy."

She laughed. "You're right. Mr. Smooth, that's what you are," she teased. "At least that's what your wife told me."

Jim made a rude noise. Penny Easton was lovely and had a great sense of humor. They had become friends despite Lyra taking her husband away so often. Jim liked to say it was so they could gang up on him.

"I know you've heard her call me that, but things change once I'm home. I can assure you that there's nothing smooth about cleaning gutters or putting out trash."

Lyra laughed, and Jim touched his cap. "Have a good evening, Ms. St. Claire."

"Stop that," she said as she went down the steps. All her staff called her Lyra when they were out of the public eye, and she wouldn't have it any other way.

His laughter followed, and the last stress of the flight slipped away—until she noticed the crowd behind the barrier.

"We changed the arrival time, so how could they know it was now?"

Maggie tutted. "You really have to ask? Symon must have found out and spread the word. 'Any exposure makes good exposure' is his motto, right?"

Lyra's stomach swirled. She tried to think the best of people, but Symon was once more not doing himself any favors. His absence was becoming glaringly obvious at the worst moments—and this was one of them. "I guess he was

87

the only one apart from us who knew about the change of plans."

"Well, it certainly wasn't me who let it slip," Maggie said wryly.

"Nor me," Dan growled.

"I never gave the notion about either of you any thought," Lyra insisted.

Dan nodded. "I guess we have no choice but to get among them unless we plan to sleep on the plane."

"I'd be game, but I'm pretty sure there's a law against it." Despite the joking, Lyra grimaced at having to run the gauntlet, then forced a smile while Dan collected their bags. Fans who'd waited around all this time to see her deserved a little attention. They didn't need to know she hated crowds and that she didn't feel up to dealing with their questions, some of which were often incredibly personal.

Symon insisted Lyra be seen as accessible, but after Duane's stalking, she'd become more adept at giving paparazzi the slip. They were the ones who bombarded her with questions about her personal life or that of the stars she interviewed. The rest of the press were less intimidating, asking questions about what she did with real interest. In the right circumstances, she could talk about recipes and cooking all day long.

Of course, there were the difficult questions from her fans regarding recipes they tried. Why they worked or failed in someone else's kitchen could only be guessed at. Still, she had to come up with a plausible answer every time to encourage them and make them feel better about their efforts. Empathy was her trademark, and incredibly tiring to portray on a day-to-day basis in case she was captured on camera.

"Lyra! Please, could I get a photo?"

A woman she recognized as a superfan waved excitedly

from the front of the crowd. If there was a chance to meet Lyra, this woman would travel miles and was one person Lyra couldn't deny a few minutes, much to the annoyance of the paparazzi who impatiently jostled the group.

"Hello, Hazel. It's lovely to see you again."

Maggie took the phone from the delighted woman's hands and snapped several shots of Hazel and Lyra. Then she stood back so the rest of the crowd could take their own. Lyra offered a few expected poses, including ones with Cinnamon, who she picked up and held to her cheek. The beagle tilted her head at the camera, and Lyra could have sworn she smiled. Cin was the one who loved the adulation, and that fact made Lyra's smile more genuine.

Maggie always knew when Lyra began to seriously struggle, and now she took her by the elbow, addressing the crowd as she propelled them all forward.

"Thanks for coming, everyone. Ms. St. Claire has had a full day. If you'll excuse her…."

Unfortunately, not everyone was as lovely as Hazel. When they went through the barrier, a microphone was thrust in Lyra's face, followed by several more. Maggie moved closer and held a hand in front of them as if that would hold them back, while Lyra looked for Symon or one of his security detail. The private airport did have security but only on-site, and they patrolled people coming into the hangar and the planes. It seemed they were on their own, and Dan had his hands full with the suitcases. Her heart pumped harder, as if she were about to take another flight.

"There's a rumor that you have a famous wedding happening at La Joliesse."

"Is there?" She blinked a couple times at the reporter for a tabloid she didn't want to be associated with. There was no way she'd divulge details of this particular wedding, to him or anybody else.

He smirked. "Are you saying there isn't?"

"I'm wondering how that became a rumor?" With an effort, her tone remained neutral. "Perhaps you know something I don't."

The microphone tapped her on the shoulder, and she flinched. Another camera flashed at that moment, taking a photo that would probably make a headline somewhere.

"Can you answer the question?" the reporter insisted.

"No, thank you. I never discuss my customers and their events or things I don't know about. Cinnamon and I thank you all for coming tonight, but we must get going."

Cinnamon gave an on-cue yap, pulling the focus from Lyra for a brief second. Maggie took the opportunity to push her way through the crowd, dragging Lyra behind her.

Lyra blew them a kiss and followed Maggie closely until they reached the car that waited out front. Dan had already stowed their bags in the trunk of the limousine he'd ordered.

"Sorry, Lyra. I didn't anticipate the lack of security or I would have left the bags until tomorrow and helped you through that lot." He nodded disdainfully at the slowly dispersing crowd, even as some of them stood a few feet away, having followed in the hopes of more details or better pictures.

Lyra might appear calm, but inside she was furious with her agent for placing her in this situation, and not for the first time. "Thanks, Dan. I also thought there'd be more security when we got out here. My mistake, apparently, but we managed thanks to Mags, didn't we, girl?"

Cinnamon yapped in agreement, and Lyra slid inside with the beagle on her lap. Maggie followed once she was sure the group outside was keeping back.

"Whew! You handled that last question well," Maggie said as she relaxed into the seat.

Lyra shook her head. "Not well enough. I wish I could lie,

but I could hardly say the celebrity wedding he was obviously referring to wasn't happening, and then several weeks later it actually does."

"Another celebrity would lie, but that's not who you are," Maggie agreed. "Perhaps a 'no comment' would be best next time, but honestly, Suki Love and Heath Carter couldn't hope for the news to stay a secret. They're ridiculously famous on their own. Together, the country's going mad for them. Bear in mind that they'll have their own stalkers and staff who could be sneaking information to the press for a bribe."

"You could be right. I do know we've been as discreet as possible with the booking. The staff at the restaurant don't even know exactly who the wedding is for. If it is coming from our end, that only leaves one person."

"We've talked about this for a while, and it finally sounds like you're ready to confront Symon." Maggie chewed her bottom lip for a second or two. "It's overdue, and we both know he's not good at hearing any complaints, so how will you handle this?"

Lyra cringed just thinking about the confrontation. "I'm not sure. I don't want the conversation to get out of hand, but I have to show him that I mean business and get him to see my point."

"You're paying him exceptionally well to represent your brand." Maggie took a deep breath. "Perhaps it's time to look for a new agent?"

Lyra knew Maggie was right. She'd known it for some time. If she didn't do something, things were unlikely to get better. Still, the idea of interviewing agents, plus attempting to filter out the potential lip service and promises from the facts like she should have done with Symon, filled her with more anxiety than having it out with him.

Maggie patted Lyra's hand. "Just know that if it goes

badly, I can take care of things until you find the right person."

Lyra smiled with relief. "Thanks, Mags. That means a lot and eases some of the pressure. It's just so difficult to trust people now that I wouldn't know where to begin. Symon's been with me practically from day one."

"Better the devil you know—is that what you're saying?" Maggie grimaced.

Lyra shrugged. "I guess. He was astute in the beginning and knew what worked for me. I've been hoping he'd turn things around and get back to that."

Maggie gave her a pitying look. "It's a shame Symon won't listen to how you want things to be or what you're prepared to do. Everyone has boundaries, and he's accepting yours less every day, but you're stronger than you think, and you shouldn't allow him to dictate your life."

Lyra squared her shoulders. Maggie was right again. It was time to make changes. She'd start by giving Symon one last chance to see sense. If he didn't, she'd deal with whatever the result was. It wasn't going to be pleasant, that much she knew.

She did feel more comfortable with her decision now because there was no denying how astute Maggie was. Using any downtime to study and being professional with any dealings, she'd cultivated many friends in the industry. They would manage just fine in the interim without an agent if that was the way the cake fell.

Dan pulled up at the hotel where they lived and, after opening the car doors, carried their bags to their rooms. Lyra was happy to be home, and Cinnamon scampered around the top-floor apartment suite, sliding on the tiled floors in her excitement.

"If you don't need me, I'm going to have a nice hot bath." Maggie stood by the door with her shoes in her hand.

Lyra chuckled. "You deserve it. Thanks for everything, and do sleep in. I'll call you later tomorrow morning."

"Thanks, boss. I hope you get a good night's sleep too."

"It's always better when I'm home." It had been weeks since they'd left LA, and Lyra was really looking forward to her own bed. Although, with all her conflicting thoughts, getting to sleep might be an issue.

Maggie left for her adjacent apartment, and Lyra took a deep breath, enjoying having familiar things around her. Close to the restaurant and her mom's retirement community apartment, the hotel suited her for the moment. Plus, having her assistant nearby was awesome.

Dan returned from the bedroom, where he'd deposited her bags, with Cinnamon in tow. "Shall I take Her Majesty for a quick walk in the park across the road?"

At the suggestion, the beagle danced around them, ready for a stroll after being cooped up for a few hours.

"That would be wonderful." Lyra gratefully handed him Cinnamon's lead. She could get a head start on unpacking while trying to formulate a plan for dealing with her agent and then call her mom.

Instead, as she removed clothes from her bag, Kaden sprang to mind. She hadn't had that much fun in a long while and had to find the time to do more than keep in touch with him. After all, what was the point of having money and fame if you lived a solitary life the way she did?

Guilt made her rethink things a little. Her mom was nearby, but Lyra was often so busy that they saw little of each other. Of course, she had to admit that the matter of the new man in her mom's life had affected how much she visited. Lyra didn't like him at all, and that was hard to hide.

Still, if he made her mom happy, then she really had to make an effort and not be so selfish.

## 12

The first thing Lyra did when she woke was ring her mom and invite her to a "girls' lunch" to avoid any chance that Mom's boyfriend might tag along and give them some much needed time together. After that she took Cinnamon for a walk and did a few chores.

At almost lunchtime, Lyra arrived at La Joliesse. Through the window, she saw waiters, led by her maître d', George Bolder, checking tables against the list of reservations. Entering the building via a private side door, she opened another door in the short hall which led to a dog-friendly patio area. This space also connected via sliding doors back into the restaurant.

George looked her way and hurried toward her. "Welcome home, Ms. St. Claire. You too, Cinnamon. I hope it was a successful trip. We certainly enjoyed coverage of the competitions."

Lyra sighed. George wasn't much older than her, and he had a charm that her customers loved. Unfortunately, like Dan, he struggled to call her Lyra even when they were alone. His excuse was that it was better to address her formally so he didn't make a mistake when it mattered. After all this time, she knew there was little point in arguing.

"Thanks, George. It was a lot of fun, and those kids certainly can cook."

She unclipped Cinnamon's leash, and the beagle went straight to the patio while George accompanied Lyra into the kitchen.

"Hello, everyone. It's so good to be home. I'll come see you all soon." Lyra waved to the chefs and assistants before following George into her office on the same side as the hall and patio. She'd designed it this way to be close enough for Cinnamon to find her, yet not have to go inside the kitchen or restaurant. Lyra also installed internal windows so that, even if she had no time to cook, she could at least see her kitchen in motion.

George took her coat and scarf and hung them just inside the office door on a wooden rack. "We've been looking forward to your return."

"No more than I have, I bet." Lyra gave a half-smile. "It's been a long few weeks."

George pursed his lips for a moment. "I hear you've had a couple of issues. Let me know if I can help with anything."

Her skin prickled at his tone. Close to Maggie, George would have heard of the death as well as the fiasco at the airport last night and everything else that had happened this trip. Lyra didn't mind, because she trusted him, but George would have a strong opinion, and she wasn't ready to get into it.

When she merely smiled her thanks, George headed back out to the restaurant. Her staff understood that she needed a few moments alone to get her bearings and check the schedule for today, and she appreciated their patience. When she wasn't here, she gave up all control to George and James Anders, her head chef. Lyra's return required an adjustment from them all, and they would have plenty to catch up on.

Lisa Moore, her accounts person, knocked and came right in. "Sorry to interrupt your quiet time, Lyra, but these need signing ASAP." She waved several papers.

"What are they?"

"Just some contracts for suppliers."

Lyra frowned. She and James had picked their suppliers carefully, wanting only the best and freshest ingredients. "I wasn't aware we were changing any."

Lisa shook her highlighted bob and smiled. "You'll have to take that up with James, I just do as I'm told."

"Leave them here, and I'll get to them by the end of the day."

"Great to have you home." With another warm smile, Lisa dropped the papers on the edge of Lyra's desk and left.

Lyra eyed a pile of messages and the contracts. The schedule was more important, so she better start with that.

Cinnamon returned from the patio and, knowing she wasn't allowed in the kitchen or restaurant, came straight to Lyra, who lifted her onto her lap in the designer chair behind the large desk.

Half an hour later, the hustle and bustle called to her stronger than ever. "I need to see my kitchen, Cin. I'll be back when I can."

She kissed her soft head, and their foreheads pressed together for a moment. Cinnamon licked her cheek, which meant Lyra had permission to leave. Lyra stood and placed the beagle back on the chair.

In the kitchen, every surface not in use gleamed as she knew it would. The sight of everyone working hard pumped her full of adrenaline, while strangely she felt at peace. This excitement and desire to cook never waned, and for the hundredth time, Lyra made a promise to herself that she would do so more often.

"Lyra." James nodded when she reached his station. From here he could watch and direct his team. He was in the zone and cooking venison, which looked delicious.

She sniffed appreciatively. "How is everything?"

"Perfect," he said with a small amount of pride and a tone that implied this outcome was the only one he would settle for.

"I knew it would be. Any issues while I was gone?"

He shrugged. "None I couldn't handle."

She nodded, not concerned with whatever he'd had to deal with. He'd tell her if he thought it necessary. Things cropped up all the time, and it was the job of the senior staff to find a work-around or to fix the issue. James made this part of her job so much easier because she didn't have to worry that La Joliesse wasn't delivering her best food every time.

So as not to destroy his focus completely, Lyra continued around the kitchen, making sure to speak to everyone. It was as important to them as it was to her that they did their jobs well. This was the culture of the restaurant, and with George and James at the helm, her standards would continue.

George bustled through the door just as she'd finished.

"Ms. St. Claire, there's a call for you. They say it's urgent and won't leave a message. I've put it through to your office," he said apologetically.

Lyra expected her staff to take messages when they could, which meant the caller was either more insistent or more important than usual. Curious, she returned to her office. Recognizing the name on the phone, she saw the video chat was blinking.

Plucking the alert Cinnamon from her chair and onto her lap, Lyra flicked the button. Movie star Suki Love appeared.

The young woman's lips quivered. "Lyra, thank goodness you're there."

"Hi, Suki. You seem upset."

The blonde bombshell was usually immaculate, but today her face was red and puffy, as if she'd been crying for some time.

Lisa chose that moment to walk into the office, and Lyra shook her head. The woman immediately shut the door behind her, understanding that the conversation must be private.

"I am. Upset and furious. We have to bring the wedding forward. Someone leaked all the details to the paparazzi, and they're hounding everyone invited to our wedding. Heath's completely over it, and I don't want the day to be a shambles. We don't know what else to do." The words tripped over themselves as the young star held back more tears.

"I'm so sorry, Suki. I'm confident it wasn't my end that leaked the date or the guest list."

"I'm sure it wasn't. Your reputation for being discreet is what made us choose you. To be honest, it was more impor-tant than the food." Suki sniffed again. "Can you help?"

Lyra opened her calendar on the laptop. "Let's see what we can do. How soon do you want to have it?"

There was a pregnant pause, then a rush of words. "In two weeks. I know it's a lot to ask. Your maître d' said there was nothing he could do, but I knew you'd help. I'll pay anything to fix this. Anything."

Lyra sucked her breath through her teeth. "You have to be kidding. George is right, the restaurant is booked solid for the next six months. I imagined you meant the change of date was bringing it forward a week or so."

The wedding of the year was supposed to be in two

months at the oldest church in LA with the reception at La Joliesse. Due to numbers, this meant closing the whole restaurant to anyone else. Lyra was willing to do so given plenty of notice. To try to cancel bookings for two weeks' time to make room would be a logistical nightmare. One Suki couldn't possibly understand or appreciate the work involved.

"I wish I was kidding. I secured a role yesterday that I want so bad. The original actress pulled out, and it's mine if I want it. I really do, Lyra. This would cement my career in a way no other role could. The start date for filming is a week later. It's either bring it forward or we hold off until afterward, but this is the third time I've delayed it. Heath thinks I don't want to marry him, but this really isn't my fault."

A small sob escaped her rosebud lips, tugging at Lyra's heart. The couple seemed so in love, and Lyra was a romantic. Although she'd never experienced true love herself. Too busy to date much, she'd never felt the urge to have second dates when there was no zing. Whatever that was.

"We can't have that. Plus, I'm sure your fans will be delighted to find out you've finally tied the knot."

Suki gave a watery smile. "That's what Heath says, and it makes sense to have the whole thing at La Joliesse, if we can. Plus, since you love pets and are dog-friendly, we can have Cutiepie come, which is so important to us."

Cutiepie was a miniature dachshund. When Lyra and Suki met at an animal shelter charity event, their dogs bonded. Adding that to the fact that they were both came from the Portland area, they became friendly, which led to the reception booking.

Suki expected Lyra to turn the reception into the whole wedding and find a space for pets. Lyra bit back a scathing remark, but there was only one option she could see, and she'd have to be firm that this was a take-it-or-leave-it scenario. Any leeway and Suki would hound her for changes.

"You've done so much for the animal shelter, and we're friends, so I'd like to help, but this is the best I can do. In two weeks, you could get married on the Monday. I'm sure it's not your preference, but just think—no one would be expecting it here because we're usually closed Mondays."

"A Monday?" The actress tapped her long red nails against the tabletop. "Why not? It'll still give us time for a short honeymoon. Let's do it! I love you!"

"You better." Lyra laughed. One could never be totally convinced that the actress was being sincere, but Lyra liked her anyway. Anyone who adored animals as much as Suki did must be a good person. "The baker and celebrant will need to be advised as well as your guests."

"The celebrant is my uncle and he'll be fine. As for the cake, could you make it, Lyra? That way it's one less place to have a leak from. I'll keep the other cake order and donate it to someone after my wedding, or the shelter could raffle it."

Lyra smothered a groan. "I will if I can. Otherwise I'll get my pastry chef on it. Either way, you'll have a cake."

Suki pouted and gave a pitiful shrug. "I guess anything will be fine."

"I'll contact you if I have any questions."

Lyra ended the call and this time groaned aloud. People made throwaway comments like that, but a movie star would expect something special. "Fine" in that tone meant settling for something substandard.

She was just about to tell James and George the news when her phone beeped. It was a message from Suki.

***By the way, there will be another twenty people. Hope that's ok. XX***

It wasn't a question, and Lyra instantly regretted her easy capitulation. The restaurant was large and had a limit of one hundred and twenty people to comply with the code. Still, one hundred people would be pushing all their reserves of tables and chairs, because Lyra liked to give her customers room to convey a sense of privacy. And the chefs—how would they cope?

She rubbed her temples, wishing she could start the day again. Then she called James and George into the office and asked them to take a seat so she could explain the situation. The men were professional, and sitting opposite her, they gave a lot of thought to resolving the issue rather than telling her how hard or impossible it was going to be.

"I'll have to see who's available, but paying the staff extra will help," James suggested.

George nodded. "It'll be a lot of work, but people respond well to bonuses. Maybe we can also get some of the setup and prep done after we close on Sunday night?"

Lyra nodded. "I'll pitch in. I've checked my calendar, and I have nothing on either day."

"That'll be a big help, and not just with another pair of hands. The chefs are inspired when they work alongside you," James said matter-of-factly.

Since he was being so positive, Lyra brought up the cake. James raised an eyebrow, which was the visible extent of his frustration.

"Anything else?"

She turned to George and grimaced. "There is the little matter of the guest list. It's now one hundred."

George whistled. "It's going to be a squeeze, in that we're recognized as being a spacious venue and we've never had that many, so we'll need extra chairs."

"I know, and I'm truly sorry. If I thought saying no wouldn't affect us, I would have. You know how celebrities are."

"Not like you."

Lyra laughed at his wink. "You have to say that. Now I know you're both discreet, but since this must be a guarded secret, let's not divulge anything until the day to the staff."

With everyone in agreement, the men hurried back to their work just as Maggie burst into the office.

"Did you hear the news?"

# 13

L yra gaped for a second. Maggie was always on top of things, but the date change had only just happened. "How did you know?"

Maggie frowned. "I got a message."

"Already? Poor Suki. I wonder if it's even worth trying for another date here."

"Pardon?"

"They wanted it kept quiet like before, and the new date was hopefully going to allow for that," Lyra explained.

Maggie looked at her as if she'd grown two heads. "I have no idea what you're talking about."

"The Love-Carter wedding. Aren't you talking about the date change?"

Maggie shook her head. "No, I'm not. What date change?"

Lyra rubbed her temples. "How about you explain what you're so fired up about first."

"Kaden Hunter."

The look of genuine sorrow on Maggie's face made the blood rush from Lyra's. "Is he okay?" she croaked.

"He is. It's his restaurant. There's been a serious fire."

C. A. PHIPPS

A restaurateur's worst nightmare, Lyra felt his pain from a state away. "I can't believe it."

Maggie pulled out her phone and showed her some pictures of Phoenix. It was still standing, only now it was marred by black walls and broken glass.

Her eyes welled up. "Poor Kaden. When did it happen?"

"This morning. I was looking up news of the wedding and those images came up. Kaden must be devastated, which is maybe why he hasn't called you."

Lyra nodded, a lump in her throat making it hard to speak. "As I would be if it happened to La Joliesse. Thanks for letting me know. I'll give him a quick call. Would you take Cin for a walk, please?"

At the W-word, Cinnamon danced at the door.

"Sure." Maggie attached her lead. "Are we still on for our meeting, or would you rather postpone it?"

"Postponing isn't an option with the changes to the wedding plans. Let's catch up over lunch. We'll have it in here, because other than you, George, and James, we don't want anyone else to know about it."

When they'd gone, Lyra steeled herself to make the video call, her heart distraught for her dear friend. It rang several times, and she'd all but given up when Kaden's face appeared before her.

"You've heard?"

His voice was flat, and her heart went out to him. "Maggie saw it on the news. I'm so sorry, Kaden. Any idea how this happened?"

His eyes narrowed. "They're treating it as arson. Looks like someone threw something down the ventilation shaft. They waited until there was no one there to notice the smoke, and the alarms were tampered with."

Lyra gasped. "Oh no. Who would want to do that?"

He shrugged, rubbing his hand through his fair hair so it stuck up in all directions.

"I've got no idea. The police asked if there was anyone who might hold a grudge against me. I truly couldn't think of a single person, but I suppose I must have annoyed someone at some time."

Unable to imagine this, Lyra croaked, "Whoever it was, I hope they catch them soon."

"Me too. Thank goodness it was after the wedding and that I'm heavily insured for fire."

No matter that he tried not to sound devastated, it was there in the white lines around his mouth and the forced crooked smile. Lyra nodded, searching for something encouraging to say that wouldn't sound trite. Then she had an idea. "Maybe this is bad timing, so tell me to get lost if you want, but I have a proposition for you."

His eyes cleared a little, giving her hope that she really could make him feel a little better.

"I'm listening."

Lyra heard the skepticism. "Whatever you need to do there, and I appreciate it won't be pleasant dealing with insurance companies, etcetera, will take time to get resolved. I have a huge wedding to cater for. It's been thrown at me for two weeks' time, and I don't have all the staff in place yet. I could really use you."

His eyes widened. "You want me to come to LA and work for you?"

She nodded enthusiastically. "If you could. I'd send the jet I lease and pay you for your time, naturally."

Kaden managed a half laugh. "Thanks, I needed that."

"I'm not joking. Actually, I could use some of your staff too. The wedding is for a hundred people."

He frowned. "Bringing us to LA seems like a lot of extra money to shell out for a wedding. Who's getting married?"

She waved a finger at him. "If I tell you, I'd have to kill you. Unless you say yes."

His eyes twinkled, but then he grimaced. "I have a lot to think about right now, what with the police and insurance. I'd hate to say yes, then let you down."

"Of course, and I didn't mean to put you on the spot. The idea just hit me, and out it came." She shrugged. "I thought I was over that."

He snorted. "Sounds like the old Lyra St. Claire, which is not a bad thing. Let me get back to you tomorrow. I'll have an idea how much I'm needed around here by then."

"Sure, and if it's no, I won't be offended. I am truly sorry that this happened to you and can only imagine how you feel."

"Thanks. I'd better go," he said hoarsely and ended the call.

Lyra squeezed her eyes tight. Crying wouldn't help, but if it was La Joliesse, she'd be curled into a ball right now in any available corner. All the celebrity shows in the world didn't come close to the feeling of owning her own restaurant, and Phoenix was as much Kaden's baby as La Joliesse was hers.

Her homecoming wasn't going as she planned, and she still had to talk to her agent and tell him a few home truths.

Lyra took several deep breaths and pulled her diary toward her. It was full, and she needed to get into working mode if she was going to make any headway.

Having written in the new date and time of the wedding using a code she'd developed out of necessity after the first time events were leaked a few months back, she pulled a pad toward her and began to jot down several things she didn't want to forget. Before Maggie returned with Cinnamon, her notes had turned into a couple of full pages.

"I hope I wasn't too long, but you know how people are when they see our girl, and we came across some children in the park."

Cinnamon loved most people, and they loved her, especially children. "The timing's perfect. Although, when you see what we have to do, you might want to run the other way."

She handed her assistant the pad and unclipped Cinnamon's leash. The beagle went straight to her water dish and then curled up under Lyra's desk.

Maggie ran her finger down each item. "It does look like a massive task, but I thought about some of this on the walk, and I think we can do it. What did the guys say?"

"Thank goodness. They feel the way you do, that we'll manage somehow."

"There you are, then. Nothing to worry about."

Lyra saw the twinkle in her friend's eyes and laughed. "What did I do to deserve you all?"

"You treat us right, and the perks aren't too shabby."

"Is that your way of saying you'd like lunch?"

Maggie winked. "Well, the rush is probably over."

Lyra intended to rustle up something when James came through the door with two fluffy omelets and bowls of salad. George followed carrying napkins, cutlery, and a jug of dressing.

"Somebody around here is reading minds." Maggie opened a small table in the corner of the room, and the men laid everything out as if they were out in the restaurant. "And I implore you to keep doing it."

Lyra laughed. "You better sit before you pass out from starvation."

The men were on their way out when Lyra called out, "How are the new suppliers going, James?"

He frowned. "Great. Is something wrong?"

"Not at all. I just wanted to make sure they were working out since we have a lot of work coming."

"There's been no problems so far."

Chefs could be a little touchy when questioned, and since James had never let her down before, Lyra readily accepted that everything was going to plan in the kitchen. "Good to know. And thanks for the lunch."

Maggie picked up her thick diary from the desk, sat down at the table, and opened it beside her. Lyra made sure Cinnamon had a doggie treat and fresh water before sitting opposite with her own diary. Working lunches were the norm for them, and often enjoyable.

They began with the change of date and quickly ran through who needed contacting to ensure they could still provide their services on such short notice. The only interruption was when George brought in coffee, and that was brief.

When they were finally up to speed, Maggie stretched. "Are you really going to do the cake yourself?"

"That depends on Kaden."

Maggie's mouth dropped open, and Lyra grinned.

"I guess I forgot to mention my conversation with him. Nothing's guaranteed, but if he can get things sorted, he may have time to come here to help with the wedding."

Maggie tilted her head. "The way you helped him?"

"Precisely."

"Only you were already there."

"True, but I had to change my flight times. The point is he needed help, and now I do."

"So, your relationship is back to how it was?"

Lyra shrugged. "We're getting there."

"He'll have a lot to deal with if it is arson."

"The fire department is pretty sure it was arson, and even

if it isn't, he'll still have insurance and tradespeople issues that might mean he can't make it. If he can, I suggested he bring some of his staff."

Maggie tapped her pen on the paper. "Did you talk to the guys about that?"

"Not yet. There hasn't been time. But I will soon. I'm sure they'll be glad for the extra hands."

Maggie nodded, but Lyra saw her worry. The business couldn't run the way it did if decisions were made without consulting her team.

"You're right. I should have mentioned it when they brought in lunch. Changing the wedding date was one thing, but bringing workers into the restaurant when they've never met and expecting George and James to accept them without question is a lot to assume."

"They're bound to understand." Maggie smiled encouragingly. "Don't beat yourself up. I know you've got a lot to think about."

Again, Lyra was reminded how fortunate she was to have such good people around her. Her fingers were firmly crossed that Kaden and his team would be available.

## 14

---

In the lull before dinner service, Lyra was on her way to talk to George and James when her phone buzzed insistently. She hurried to her desk, expecting another text from Suki. Instead, she saw it was a message from Kaden. If he'd made up his mind so soon, it couldn't be good news.

*Yes.*

Lyra stared at the word, rubbed her eyes once, twice. Then her fingers flew across the buttons.

*Seriously? You're coming to help me out?*

Kaden answered right away.

*Why not? Nothing's going to happen here until the adjusters get back to me. Then they'll fight to not pay out. A battle will unfold, so working will help take my mind off it.*

*Good, and the timing is perfect.*

There were a few seconds of radio silence. Lyra reread her text and gasped at her insensitivity, quickly adding, *I didn't mean to make light of what's happened. This wedding needs another chef, especially one of your caliber.*

*I get it. By the way, Colin and Angela just stopped by to see if they could help and I suspect to check on me, which was kind of them. Anyway, I'm looking forward to coming to cook with you.*

She breathed a sigh of relief. *I'm glad. And the others? After seeing him in action, I know I could use Colin, and Angela seems to have a great rapport with customers.*

*Are you kidding? Colin was pretty excited at working with the famous Lyra St. Claire, but Angie all but jumped out of her skin!*

*Fantastic. I'll take care of the accommodation right away and send the plane when you're ready. Maggie will email you the details.*

*Talk soon.*

Placing the phone on her desk, Lyra swung her chair 360 degrees, making Cinnamon bark from under the desk. Lyra made a soothing noise and scratched between the beagle's perky ears. As sad as she was for Kaden, this wedding looked like it was going to work out better than expected.

Not having to chase extra staff also gave her a little breathing space, and since she was on a roll, she decided to use the time to deal with Symon. The conversation they needed to have wouldn't get easier by putting it off.

A pain in her stomach made her lean back and do a few breathing exercises. Symon shouldn't tie her up in knots this way. She was his boss, and she dealt with all her other staff firmly and she hoped fairly, so why was he any different? No longer the timid chef in all things except cooking, it was time Symon understood that she'd grown up and wasn't going to accept his blasé treatment of her or rudeness to people she cared about.

Taking a deep breath, she sent him a message to meet her in the park down the road from the restaurant in two hours. It was also near to her apartment—just in case she needed to escape in a hurry. The park would be quiet at this time of the

BEAGLES LOVE CUPCAKE CRIMES

day and, more importantly, neutral ground. She didn't want him in her home or at the restaurant if he was going to turn nasty.

Her phone beeped almost immediately.

*I was about to call you, but that suits me fine. I'm looking forward to seeing you and hearing all your news. X*

Getting back to her so fast was unusual and her fault. Before today, she had allowed him to dictate when and where their meetings would take place. Even that "kiss" at the end made her squirm, but at least he didn't attempt to negotiate to suit himself. She intended to go to their meeting with facts and keep her anger under wraps. She would contact her lawyer first and make sure she had all bases covered just in case it turned ugly.

But first, she had to talk to her team about the likelihood of Kaden and a few of his staff arriving. She carried the dirty cups to the dishwasher and placed them inside.

George hurried over. "You should have called for someone to clear them."

"I can clean up my own mess. Plus, I needed a word with you and James."

His smile faltered. "More bad news?"

"Hopefully the opposite."

He called James over, and they went back into her office, where she told them her plan.

"I'm sorry for dropping it on you this way. I should have asked what you thought first."

James shrugged. "In my opinion, there's nothing negative about this. We'll need extra staff, and if they're as competent as you say, then we all win."

Lyra grinned. "You have no idea how relieved I am."

"I wish you knew how much credibility you have with us," George said.

A lump formed in her throat. "Thanks for the vote of

confidence. I have a difficult meeting soon, and you've made the prospect more palatable."

"Is it the press? Do you have Dan or Maggie going with you?"

She smiled at his concern. "Nothing like that, George. I'm meeting Symon."

"Then you definitely need backup," he retorted.

"I'll be fine, but thanks again for your support."

They went back to work, but she noticed as she spoke to her lawyer that both men stopped by more frequently to check on her.

Once she hung up from the call that reassured her of the best way to handle Symon, her phone rang again. The number was unknown, and she toyed with the idea of not picking up but was glad she did.

"Ms. St. Claire? I can't believe you answered. It's Cameron Willett. Remember me?"

She laughed. "Hi, Cameron. Of course I remember you. How are things?"

"Great, thanks. This is a bit embarrassing, but I can't reach anyone to ask about the prizes I won. Sorry, but I don't know who else to contact."

Symon had clearly mucked up again. "That's no good. Don't worry, I'll get my assistant on it first thing tomorrow."

"Thank you so much. Ahhh, if it's not too rude, I was also wondering if you had any jobs available?"

"It's not rude at all." In fact, she admired him for asking. "Unfortunately, it wouldn't be right to take on other contestants, but if I hear of an opening elsewhere, would you like me to call you?" Symon would be furious, but for once, she would do what she wanted.

"Thank you so much. I'll wait to hear from Maggie, then."

She heard the disappointment and wished she could offer

him a job but that would set a precedent she couldn't allow. "Good luck and take care, Cameron."

Hopefully, he would get a chance very soon to show how good he was.

## 15

S lipping on a beige coat and the obligatory scarf, Lyra headed out for her meeting with Symon. It was getting too warm for this getup, but being in a public place, she needed to be even less conspicuous than usual.

She didn't have to say a word to Cinnamon. Alerted to them going out by a coat leaving its peg, the beagle waited patiently at the door, the lead in her mouth.

Lyra hesitated as they stepped outside. Symon wasn't the easiest person to get a point across to because he thought he knew best—always. Frankly, his powers of persuasion bordered on bullying.

Cinnamon growled.

Lyra narrowed her eyes as a man darted around the rear of the building. The paparazzi knew she was back in LA, so it could be one of them. Except they didn't usually run the other way as soon as they saw her. Which meant there was someone else involved in tracking her every move. She closed her eyes and tried to conjure up who it could be. The dark gray coat hid everything but the bottoms of jeans, and a cap covered his hair. He wore sunglasses, which covered his face, though from so far away, she couldn't have picked up features anyway. It definitely wasn't Duane because the build was too slim.

A hand on her shoulder made her gasp.

"Sorry, I didn't mean to startle you." George studied her intently. "You've been standing there a while. Are you okay?"

"I saw someone near the corner, but they're gone now. It could simply be someone in a hurry and I'm being overly suspicious."

"Sure, and nothing has happened lately to warrant you being cautious." George shook his head and took her arm. "I'll walk you to the meeting."

"You've got too much to do." She tried to pull away, but George pursed his lips and held on. If this had been Symon, she'd be furious, but George's sincerity was never in question.

"Well, maybe to the street," she conceded. "I'm meeting Symon in the park, so I'll be fine there."

They walked quickly, entering the main street, and turned right. George checked every doorway plus both sides of the street, and Lyra noticed he wore no sweater. When they got to the next intersection, she pulled her arm from his. "This is far enough."

"Are you sure?"

She nodded. "Absolutely. We're not far from the park."

"Will you let me know if you go home or if you're coming back to the restaurant?"

"I usually keep you informed."

He raised an eyebrow. "Nothing is usual lately, and I'm happy to come and meet you."

"That won't be necessary, but if it makes you feel better, I promise to message you either way."

"It does." George smiled and headed back down the street.

Apparently it wasn't just Lyra who was uneasy these days.

She had to admit it did feel good to have people in her corner who cared and she trusted. Once, Symon fit in that group, but sadly no longer.

Head high, she marched determinedly with Cinnamon trotting beside her until they entered the park.

"Lyra!" Symon waved from where he sat on a bench roughly ten feet away. He jumped up and came toward them.

His car hadn't been on the road, so he must have come in from the other side, where she lived. Nervously, she glanced around. There were a few moms or nannies with strollers and a couple joggers, but they weren't near the bench. This place was as good as any to have a tricky conversation.

"How are you, Symon?" As hard as she tried, her smile felt unnatural, and Cinnamon growled as soon as he got close. Lyra stood between them.

"Wonderful, especially now that we're together again." He took her hand without the lead, squeezing it firmly, and kissed her cheek.

It took a good deal of resolve not to wipe her skin.

"It might have only been a couple days, but I've missed you," he continued, oblivious to her discomfort.

"Can we sit for a minute?" she asked, pulling her hand from his.

"Of course. Are you tired?"

Surprised that he'd bothered to ask, she shook her head. "Not especially. Although, it's been a busy time, and I'm glad to be home for a while. What about you? What have you been up to?"

He paled. "Me? What do you mean?" Guilt suffused his face, and he plonked down beside her, pulling at the neck of his shirt as though it was suddenly too tight.

"Is there something you want to tell me? Something you should say but think it's better I don't know about?" she asked candidly.

121

"I'm sure I have no idea what you're talking about."

His huffiness rang a few more bells, and she sighed. There was no right way to begin. Half turning so she could look at him directly, she kept her voice even. "Symon, I'm not happy with the way things are going. Lately you've made decisions I object to, and you aren't taking my thoughts on them seriously."

He patted her hand. "Sweetness, I'm not sure what's gotten into you, but I'm your agent. You pay me to know my job inside and out, and I do. Haven't I done well for you so far?"

For the second time, she pulled her hand from under his and onto her lap. "I'm not disputing that you've helped me to get me where I am, and I'm grateful. It's recent issues I have a problem with. The way you seem to think my brand is heading is not where I want it to go. And when I need security, I want to have it and not be vulnerable just so you can get my name in the news."

His eyes narrowed. "Maybe I've made a couple errors, but we always manage to fix them without any hassle."

"Actually, that's the point of this meeting. There have been too many 'hassles' lately. I appreciate that things can't always go completely to plan, but if I hadn't had Maggie with me last night, things may have gotten out of hand. The 'we' you talk about never came into the equation, because you weren't there to help or witness it."

He sniffed. "You're being melodramatic. Something came up that I couldn't get out of."

Lyra shifted uncomfortably. She disliked the dismissive manner he developed whenever she questioned him. "I told you I wanted a quiet homecoming. While I want to believe that whatever you were doing was on my behalf, that's no excuse for not having any security."

He shrugged, ignoring the dig that he had someone on his books who was more important.

"You don't always understand what's needed. It was an opportunity for your local fans to get up close. Besides, Dan was there."

Her anger was about to explode, and she had to take a couple deep breaths. "That's not his job, and since you didn't know how many people were going to turn up, he might not have been enough."

Symon grinned, stretching his legs out in front of him, ankles crossed. "But it worked out perfectly. You got good exposure in the papers, and no one was hurt."

Lyra had officially had enough of his dismissiveness and his ego. She needed to wipe the smug look off his face. "That's not good enough, Symon. Not good enough at all. I was scared, and if that counts for nothing, then I guess it's time we accept that we have different ideas and agendas for my career and move on."

His grin slipped a little. "You know that's not true. I'm your biggest fan and supporter. Everything I do is for you."

The saccharine in his voice made her stomach churn. Had he always been like this, and somehow she'd been blind to it? Or had familiarity really bred contempt?

"I think it used to be, but not anymore." She stood and looked down at him. "As much as I'm grateful for all you've done for me in the past, I'm done talking about this."

He leaped to his feet, and Cinnamon bared her teeth, emitting a long, low growl. Taking a step back, Symon glared at Lyra and her dog, cementing his dismissal.

"Don't be ridiculous. You need me now just as much as you did back at the start."

She raised an eyebrow at his inability to admit there was a problem and that it stemmed from him. "I'm willing to try without you because I can't and won't accept working with someone who doesn't respect me."

He didn't back down. "You're behaving like a diva. No one will hire you without an agent."

Her jaw ached from clenching her teeth, and she chose to ignore the diva dig. "If there's a choice over privacy and safety, while preserving my integrity, I have my restaurant to fall back on. I'd be happy to have it as my main focus. Plus, Maggie can cover your role until I hire someone else if that proves necessary."

He snorted. "You'd get bored without the shows, and Maggie hasn't got a clue about what I do to keep you a star."

Lyra dug her fingernails into her free palm. "That's okay with me. I really won't mind if all I am is a chef."

He blustered. "You're in a snit. I'll give you time to calm down, and then we can talk like rational adults. I'll call you tomorrow."

Blood flushed her face and pounded at her temples. "Please don't bother. This is goodbye, Symon. You should contact Maggie to finalize any outstanding shows and to hand over anything relevant to my career."

"You can't do this. We have a contract."

His eyes glistened, and something like panic flashed across his face. It was obviously sinking in that this was the end of the road, and though Lyra had a rush of guilt, she held fast. If she gave in now, they would be back to square one, and she didn't want to ever have to do this again.

"My lawyer will be in touch with yours to make this as painless as possible. Good luck for the future, Symon, and thank you for all you've done."

She walked away, her stomach fighting to keep its contents. Never had she been so blunt with another person, but one thing Symon had taught her was never to burn bridges. To be fair, he'd also taught her how to cope with life in the spotlight, and she was truly thankful for that.

Cinnamon bumped her legs and gave a whimper.

"I'm fine, Cin. If all goes to plan, we don't have to see him again."

Lyra checked her watch. The horrible meeting took less than half an hour, so she decided to go back to work. Halfway there, her phone beeped, and she stopped to read the message.

**It's best that you go home if you can. There's a swarm of press outside the restaurant. They might head to your place when they find out you're not here.**

George's warning made her turn tail. When they realized she wasn't at La Joliesse, they would probably try the apartment, but they'd never gain access. At least they wouldn't be camped outside the restaurant and hinder the staff or put off diners. It also meant she'd be stuck there.

Had Symon set her up to be mobbed on her return?

Furious again, she took a cab to her mom's, making a call to Maggie on the way after texting George to tell him her plans.

Patricia St. Claire opened the door excitedly. "Hello, darling girl. Did I get our family time and the date mixed up?"

"No, I'm afraid I'm hiding out."

Mom frowned. "Whatever from? The paparazzi again?"

Lyra grimaced. "Yes, but I had a run-in with Symon. It wasn't pleasant. I fired him."

"Well done! I never liked that man." Mom sniffed as she removed her bright yellow apron.

The vehement reaction shocked Lyra, and she dropped onto the sofa. "You never told me that."

"Do you like him?" Mom smiled like a cat while rubbing Cinnamon's belly.

"I guess not," she admitted. "Can I hang out with you for a while?"

"You never have to ask. I love to see you any time. Archie will be back for his dinner soon. Will you stay to eat?" Mom laughed. "Obviously it can't compare to your cooking, but you always liked it."

Somehow Lyra had forgotten about the boyfriend, and she had to muster a smile. "Thanks for the offer, but I'll be gone by then."

"I understand. That fancy restaurant needs you, and you've only just got home."

Lyra didn't argue that James and George had things under control. She would enjoy a little time with her mom instead of worrying about Symon. Or Archie. The so-called actor, who never seemed to work, lived off her mom, and asked far too many questions about Lyra and money.

Plus, Cinnamon was very wary around him.

## 16

The next morning, Maggie arrived early at Lyra's apartment. With a grim expression, bypassing the usual hug and Cinnamon's customary scratch, Maggie laid a newspaper on the dining table. The beagle trailed hopefully behind her without success.

"Cinnamon isn't herself this morning. Until now, she's moped around the apartment, sniffing everywhere. If she doesn't perk up a bit more, I'll take her to the V-E-T."

"Poor baby. Is that right?" Maggie made a fuss but was obviously distracted.

"Okay, what's happened now?"

Maggie gave her an apologetic look and opened the paper to page two. She tapped a large photo. Lyra and Kaden were front and center, hugging with their eyes closed. In stark contrast, underneath this was a photo of Lyra and Symon standing toe to toe. He wore a look of surprise while she had anger written all over her face. Worst of all was the photo beside that. It showed Adam kissing her onstage at the awards.

"Anyone could have taken the first two and sold them to

the press. The one with Symon had to be someone following you," Maggie said through gritted teeth.

"I was sure I'd seen someone hanging around the restaurant!" Lyra's outrage matched her assistant's and escalated when she read the caption.

*"Chef and show host joins lover in Portland—or should that be lovers? Lyra St. Claire immediately returned to spurn her long-term boyfriend in LA. Agent to the stars, Symon Reeves is devastated at being publicly dumped without warning. He had no comment on Ms. St. Claire's morals."*

Lyra clenched her fists. The private moment between her and Kaden was taken at the wedding. Therefore, there were plenty of people with the ability to take photos and sell them. Just as there were at the awards.

She leaned over them. The picture in the park had to have been taken by a professional. The grainy shot implied that it was taken from a good distance away, which made it easy to put two and two together and come up with Symon as the culprit. No, he didn't take any of them, but he'd certainly be delighted for them to be printed in the manner they were.

"We've never been involved. I bet this is the work of Symon's sneaky photographer!"

Maggie tapped the page once more, and Lyra read the name under the pictures. Duane Buchanan—just as she suspected.

"He loves to stir up trouble for me, and now it makes sense why. He's on Symon's payroll, and the reporter must be too. That explains a lot about my recent publicity. These guys don't have to do any work to locate me because all the information is handed to them on a plate."

"Which means he's paying the guy with your money. It's obvious Symon wants to discredit you before the news gets out about why you fired him." Maggie smirked. "Still, as much as it stinks, I doubt this story will work the way he imagines."

"How so?"

"People think of you as star royalty. You have tons of fans dying to know if you have a boyfriend, because they like to see the princess marry the prince."

Lyra frowned. "But I don't have a boyfriend, and I certainly wouldn't want anyone to think that I am, or was, romantically involved with Symon. Besides, Kaden doesn't need the press hounding him about a harmless hug between friends right now."

"Well, I think the saying 'any publicity is good publicity' applies here—for you and Kaden. It keeps his restaurant on the map while he rebuilds it, which has to be good for business, and will do the same for you if you don't have a show for a while."

Lyra understood what Maggie was saying, but it still didn't feel right. "I don't like lying."

"You did nothing to add to this story, so you're not the liar, right?"

"If someone asks, I'll have to refute it."

Maggie rolled the paper and dumped it in the trash. "Agreed, if you get asked outright, but we don't have to offer the information anytime soon. Meanwhile, you and Kaden get a little free publicity that we hadn't counted on, and Symon's still fired."

"Put like that, it does sound like a win-win situation." Lyra grimaced. "I guess trying to deny it will only encourage the paparazzi. Anyway, are you interested in how it went with Symon?"

Maggie raised an eyebrow. "When you called me yesterday afternoon, I was on cloud nine and I told you we should celebrate the split. You were the one feeling bad and didn't want to go into details."

"It was pretty ugly, but I feel a darn sight better this morning." She glanced at the trash and screwed up her nose. "I just wish it hadn't come to that showdown. You didn't see the anger in his eyes."

"I've seen it before, directed at me. Symon wants to be the big cheese, and everyone else is dirt on his shoe. He had to hide that from you because you pay his bills. By the way, did you find out why the paparazzi were at the restaurant yesterday?"

"They saw a picture of Kaden and me during the wedding at Phoenix with the mayor's family. According to George, they had a lead that I was working there and was considering buying his restaurant before it was burned down because Kaden's in financial trouble."

"Is he?"

"Not as far as I know."

"No prizes for guessing Symon's had a hand in that too. Did you hear them outside here last night? Security called the police, and they were moved on pretty quickly."

"I had my headphones on to calm myself down." Lyra sighed. "The press are causing disruptions more frequently, and it isn't fair to the other residents or staff. I'd better apologize to the manager and send gift baskets again."

Maggie raised an eyebrow. "That's only putting a Band-Aid on the situation. We've discussed this many times, but I really think it's time to get your own place."

Lyra sighed. "It is, but what's put me off is finding a discreet agent and having the time to look."

"Let's go over what you need, and I'll find the agent. Then I'll make a short list so you're not traipsing around...."

"That makes sense," Lyra agreed, but Maggie was suddenly wide-eyed. "What's the matter?"

"Your laptop!" Maggie hurried to the kitchen counter. "Did you have an accident?"

Lyra's bag was upturned, and her laptop lay beside it in two pieces. It was a vital piece of equipment that was never out of her sight. Along with her diary, she kept information on it for everything she did. Plus, it held every recipe she'd ever made or planned to make in the future. How had she not noticed the state of it?

Her hands hovered over the smashed screen. "It was fine last night. I used it after I got home until dinner. I made an omelet and ate at the counter. It was perfectly fine then. There's only one plausible answer." Cinnamon whined and stood on her hind legs to sniff at the counter. A low growl rumbled from her chest, and Lyra appreciated the sentiment. "Someone came in here last night."

"How come Cinnamon didn't warn you?"

"Good point, Mags. I listened to an audiobook in bed using my earbuds, so if she did do anything other than bark, perhaps I wouldn't have noticed." Even as she said this, Lyra doubted the possibility. Cinnamon always alerted her to visitors, whether she knew them or not.

Maggie frowned. "The rooms are pretty soundproof, but I don't accept that. I think we should check the rest of the apartment."

Imagining someone snooping around in here, Lyra suddenly had a horrible thought and ran to her bedroom. On the bedside table was her diary. Clasping it to her chest, she smiled at Maggie, who'd followed her. "Thank goodness I had this with me. I planned to go over a few things but fell asleep."

"Hopefully that means they got nothing because you had Cinnamon in there with you. I'll check the other rooms while you call the police."

Lyra made the call, sighing when she was done. "The police have a car in the area, but it's not a priority since no one's hurt. While we wait, I'm going to check out the rest of the apartment."

Maggie went with her. When they were done and found no evidence, or intruder, she touched Lyra's shoulder. "Whatever the police say, you have to stay somewhere else tonight."

Lyra slumped onto a dining chair, her mind reeling. "The door hasn't been tampered with. Therefore, if someone got in here once, they can do it again. And there's something else."

Maggie sat beside her. "Go on."

"I was feeling vulnerable yesterday, and angry that Symon knows more about my life than I do. I have no doubt that he'll cause waves to teach me a lesson."

"He can be vindictive," Maggie agreed.

"As soon as I got home, I changed all my passwords. Whoever came in here was after something on my laptop and they couldn't get it."

"Symon," Maggie hissed. "While I'm glad he didn't get anything, you're lucky he didn't take it out on you."

Lyra didn't believe Symon broke into her apartment. He hired people to do the less savory jobs, as she well knew. But whoever broke in could have attacked or killed her, and that was more sobering than anything else.

A firm knock at the door filtered through her sickening thoughts.

## 17

Maggie led two police officers to where Lyra waited by the counter. The male officer didn't wait for an introduction as Cinnamon danced around his feet. She was clearly feeling much better.

"Ms. St. Claire, I'm Officer Denton, and this is Officer Shaw."

He was a middle-aged fatherly looking figure, while Shaw was a pretty early-twentysomething who blushed and stared at both Lyra and the dog as if she couldn't believe it was them.

"Cin, come and sit." The beagle did as she asked, slumping her nose onto her front paws in disappointment, which made the young officer smother a laugh. "Thank you for coming so quickly. I appreciate how busy you are."

Officer Denton nodded, pretending to ignore Cinnamon, who sniffed at him, but he definitely had a twinkle in his eye. "You've had a break-in?"

Standing at Lyra's side, Maggie pointed to the laptop. "As far as we know, this is the only thing that's broken or touched, and we don't think anything's been taken."

"And you are?"

"I'm Lyra's personal assistant, Maggie Parker."

"And good friend," Lyra added.

"But you don't live here?"

"No. I live in the apartment next door. When I arrived this morning, neither of us had any idea someone had been in here apart from Lyra."

"I see. This laptop, it's important?"

"It contains my life," Lyra replied.

Officer Shaw gasped, then covered it with a cough.

Lyra gave a wry smile. "What I mean is that every recipe I've invented and others to be tested are on there. It also contains all documents and dealings with guests, my producer, and clients. These are all confidential."

Officer Denton nodded thoughtfully. "I appreciate that, but we may need to know more about these dealings in the future. The names would be useful now, just in case."

Lyra was prepared to give them as much information as she remembered, but couldn't get her head around someone coming into her apartment and Cinnamon not being aware of it.

Someone wanted something on her laptop, and they would have gotten it but for what she thought was her paranoia about changing passwords. How would they deal with the failure?

"What would be the benefit of this information?" Officer Denton asked.

"There's so much on it that I can't say what would be of most interest without knowing what the person wanted it for. I was uneasy last night and fortunately decided to change all my passwords."

He raised an eyebrow. "So you already suspected that someone might try to gain access from this laptop. Anyone in particular?"

Lyra didn't appreciate his tone. "All I know is that after meeting with my agent, it made me feel better to make the changes."

"So, you were furious with your agent for his alleged behavior, and you changed your passwords because you felt threatened by him?" Officer Denton pressed.

"He had access to all my accounts, emails, and contacts, as well as my diary. Like I said—my life."

"Changing passwords is standard practice when someone leaves employment," Maggie interjected.

He frowned at her and directed another question to Lyra. "Did you happen to check your accounts this morning?"

Her mouth opened and closed a few times, and Lyra felt sick again.

Without asking, Maggie opened her bag and placed her laptop in front of Lyra. "Use mine. I'm sorry I didn't think about this earlier."

No one spoke as Lyra's trembling fingers loaded the app and typed in her password. Her fingers scrolled the accounts, and finally she let out the breath she'd held. "Everything looks right."

"Then there's just the matter of a broken laptop," Denton said dismissively.

"And the break-in," Lyra reminded him.

"As there's no forced entry, we can only assume that the person had access." Denton frowned. "It is odd that your dog wasn't alerted."

Lyra also struggled to understand why Cinnamon hadn't made a fuss. "I agree. She has perfect hearing and is usually a great guard dog, but she's a little under the weather, which could explain things." She felt her eyes widen. "Or maybe the intruder knows her."

"That's a good point. How many people have a key to your apartment?"

"It's not a proper key—there's a keypad instead. Aside from me, Symon and Maggie are the only ones who have the code, along with the hotel manager, who personally lets in the cleaning staff three times a week. Yesterday wasn't a cleaning day."

"That narrows it down." The officer glanced at Maggie. "We'll speak to the manager after this. The problem with the other two is that if both of them have touched your laptop and have access to your apartment, then fingerprinting isn't an option as they'll already be there. With no fingerprints and no proof, the only thing we can do is to ascertain their whereabouts last night."

Lyra didn't like the way he was looking at Maggie. "The staff here are wonderful, and my assistant is above suspicion."

Officer Denton stood. "I'm afraid no one falls into that category until we prove otherwise. We'll be going, but please let us know if you discover anything else is amiss."

Maggie saw them out, and Lyra managed a smile for Officer Shaw, who all but fell out the door where Dan waited like a sentinel. Maggie insisted on calling him after she'd called the police, and Lyra, convinced there was more than Symon involved, was glad of his presence. Once the police spoke with Symon, he'd be alerted that she suspected him. Fear gripped her as she imagined repercussions, and suddenly she was angry again.

Pacing the room, Lyra fumed. "I'm no clearer why someone wanted my laptop if it wasn't to access my accounts. The recipes could be worth something, but only in the right hands."

"You do interview some important people, and your itinerary was in the calendar," Maggie pointed out.

"True. Which rules out Symon, because he already knows my every move."

"It might if that was the reason," Dan said skeptically.

Cinnamon woofed and paced at the door, overdue for her morning walk.

"Poor, Cin." Lyra grabbed her coat. "You've been so patient."

Dan shook his head. "You shouldn't go out alone."

"Don't you think that's a little over the top?"

His lips pursed. "Not after seeing that smashed laptop."

"If they'd wanted to harm me, they could have done so while I slept."

"Just for a while, let Dan or me come with you," Maggie pleaded. "Or let us take her. At least until we see what Symon's or one of his cohort's next move is."

Lyra could see how worried they were, but as much as she appreciated this, it didn't help her confusion. "I can't understand why he'd be involved in something like this."

"Unfortunately, I can," Maggie said grimly. "He's just lost a rather substantial meal ticket, and that wouldn't sit well with him."

Lyra thought about that for a minute. "Okay, he's desperate, but what's his motive? He can't think a stunt like this would get him back in my good graces. Unless he's thinking of some form of blackmail or that it would make me think I need his protection." She shook her head. "Whatever the reason, he would know he'd be the number one suspect. If scaring me was what he wanted, he certainly succeeded, but that doesn't seem enough to run the risk of being caught." Though she'd spoken aloud, Lyra's mind was in overdrive searching through all the possible answers. Nothing jumped out as plausible.

Maggie sighed. "He wanted you under his thumb. It's what he's always wanted. Since you began to push back, he became totally unreasonable. He gambled with the wrong celebrity."

Dan glared at Maggie but spoke to Lyra. "I wish you'd leave it to the police to work out."

"I know I should, but you heard Officer Denton. He doesn't think he can prove anything."

He crossed his arms. "What are you suggesting? Chasing Symon down and questioning him yourself?"

"I wouldn't have to chase him anywhere. I'd simply call and ask if he knows anything about this." The idea made Lyra uneasy, but she couldn't sit around waiting for the next event.

"How would that help? You've seen him in action. The man could lie his way out of court."

"So, I should do nothing?"

"My honest opinion is to wait and see what his next move is," Dan said earnestly. "You don't want to encourage him in any way to have contact with you."

"I agree," Maggie added. "When Symon wants something, he doesn't like to give up. He'll try again without you saying a word."

"I don't like it." Lyra sighed. "But I guess it would be pointless to speak to him when I made it clear that I wouldn't. It would almost be a backward step, and I don't want to give Symon any power over me ever again."

"I'm so glad." Dan gave a wry grin. "Now you just have to tell George. If you think I'm overreacting, he'll have you handcuffed to him."

Lyra groaned as they headed out the door with a desperate pooch. Her freedom from Symon was coming at a very high price.

In fact, it didn't feel like freedom at all.

# 18

It was two days later when, feeling trapped at her desk, Lyra got another message from Kaden. Waiting on the insurance and unable to do more about his restaurant just now, he was keen to help her out.

Immediately she messaged him back, asking him to let Maggie know when he'd like to come so she could arrange transport. Her assistant had picked up the reins that Symon unwillingly dropped and was doing a great job despite the loss of support from some of the agent's contacts. The varying reasons they weren't committing to more shows right now did not sit well with Lyra or Maggie.

Lyra didn't regret firing him, but her life had changed, and she was tense because of it. The first night after the break-in, she stayed at Maggie's. The key code was changed immediately, and the manager agreed to beef up security, so she went back to her apartment the next evening. She'd told Maggie and Dan it was what she wanted, which was a lie. This was more about not giving in to the fear rather than feeling safe, but she wasn't sure the fear would ever go away.

Symon hadn't been in contact despite Lyra knowing he

was questioned by the police. And now it was as if she was waiting for something awful to happen, with no idea of when or what it might look like.

While grateful for Maggie's and Dan's concern, Lyra's frustration grew at never being alone unless she was in bed. Cinnamon didn't mind the extra company, but she too was anxious over the change to their routine. Which was why Lyra sent Maggie to look for a new apartment.

Lyra stared out to the kitchen where her staff were working hard. Cinnamon nuzzled her hand, and she leaned down to hug her. "I've so much to be grateful for and I have to get out of this funk."

Cinnamon gazed at her lovingly and woofed gently.

"I need to focus on something else, and goodness knows there are plenty of other things that need my attention."

The head tilt followed by another woof motivated Lyra to go through her to-do list once more.

An hour later her phone buzzed, and she grinned at the text from Kaden. *Finally, some good news.*

*Colin, Angie, and I are headed to the airport. I hope you don't mind, but you did say come when we could. Maggie already called to say your pilot is on his way. Talk about traveling in style! We're looking forward to the break and are itching to see La Joliesse in person. Did you manage to find us a place to stay? If not, just point us in the direction of a reasonable hotel. See you in a few hours.*

She replied instantly.

*Fantastic! Accommodation is sorted. See you soon. X*

It wasn't a lie. Maggie had already told her that everything was under control, and to prove the point, a message from her assistant popped up to confirm everything.

Just hearing from Kaden helped ease the hurt and anger over Symon. It would be so good to have her friend by her side again. With enthusiasm for the reunion restoring her good humor, Lyra was ready to tackle the last details for the celebrity wedding, relieved to think of something positive.

"Is that a smile?" George leaned against the open door.

"I need to get home and do a few things before your extra team members arrive today."

His frown was deep. "Today? The wedding's not until the weekend."

"After all the drama over the fire, maybe they need to get away. I guess they'll sightsee until you need them." Lyra snorted. "Although, knowing Kaden, and watching Colin at work, I suspect they'll want to spend time here to see how we do things."

George's reply was cagey at best. "I suppose that's a good thing."

"You're in charge here," she reminded him. "There's no need to be apprehensive. Kaden and his team might be awesome, but they understand their roles and will be happy to take directions."

George flushed a little, then laughed. "If you vouch for them, I'm sure it'll be fine. By the way, I had to have a word with the staff about feeding Cinnamon. I found another cupcake on the patio this morning. Luckily it was before you arrived."

"They all know the policy around her." Lyra stiffened. "Wait, what do you mean by 'another cupcake'?"

"There was one a couple days ago. That time I caught Ms. Cinnamon eating it." His smile slipped. "She didn't eat much of it. I thought they all understood, and if I find out who it was, there will be trouble."

Lyra's mouth tightened. "Let them know it is now a sackable offence. That was the night I had the intruder. Cinnamon was very sick and didn't react, and now I know why. It was lucky she didn't die."

He paled. "I didn't put the two together. I'm so sorry."

She rubbed a hand across her face. "It's not your fault. I'm sure you saved her life when you took the rest from her. I can't thank you enough, George."

He nodded, only slightly mollified. "I'll get Dan to take you home."

Cinnamon was at the door before Lyra stood, but she didn't make it more than a few steps before the beagle growled. George was returning and had Officers Denton and Shaw with him.

"They would like a word," he said apologetically.

She waved them inside. "Please come in and have a seat. Is there news about the break-in?"

The officers remained standing with serious expressions. "Not yet, and that's not why we're here." Officer Denton nodded toward Officer Shaw, who held out a photo.

"Do you know this man?"

Lyra recognized him immediately. "That's Adam Lancaster. He won the Best Young Chef of the Year award a week or so back."

"When was the last time you saw him?"

"It was on the night of the awards. Is he all right?"

Officer Denton ignored her question. "You didn't leave with him that night?"

"I left with my assistant."

"Are you in a relationship with Adam Lancaster?"

Lyra reared back. "I certainly am not."

"We have it on good authority that you went on a date with him."

"Then your source is mistaken. It was a publicity stunt dinner organized by my agent, Symon Reeves."

Officer Denton raised an eyebrow. "Your agent?"

It stood to reason that the police would have seen the photos in the paper, but the officer's attitude implied that she was lying, and her words came out through gritted teeth. "I mean my ex-agent. And before you ask, no, we are not, nor have we ever been, an item either."

"The papers—"

"The papers, not for the first time, are wrong." Lyra's anger boiled, and it was an effort to keep her cool. "I am not in a relationship with anyone and haven't been in one for years."

Denton raised an eyebrow. "On your last trip there, when did you leave Portland?"

"The next evening after the competition. I used a leased plane and worked all day in my friend's restaurant to help him out. I'm sure you can confirm this by accessing the pilot's records and logged flight plan."

"This friend, would that be Kaden Hunter?"

"That's right. I've known him for years. We trained together. Look, what is this about?"

Officer Denton took his time answering, watching her closely. "Adam Lancaster was found dead last night."

Lyra dropped into her chair. "I can't believe it. But what does this have to do with me?"

"We checked his phone and he called you several times, didn't he?"

She blanched. "Oh. That's right. I never answered any of them."

"Why was that?"

"Because I told him often enough that I wasn't interested in furthering our relationship. In fact, after the stunt he pulled by kissing me for the paparazzi's benefit, which was pure sensationalism, I refused to speak to him again unless it was to do with the contest. Clearly, since you're asking these questions, his death is suspicious, but I don't understand why you'd think I had anything to do with it. I was here, not in Portland last night."

Officer Denton watched her closely. "We found Mr. Lancaster last night but he died several days ago."

She gasped. "I can assure you, I did not see Adam after the contest."

He merely continued. "Did you know he was in love with you?"

She shook her head. "That's not true. We hardly knew each other."

"Perhaps he was infatuated," Officer Shaw said and received Denton's glare.

"Whatever it was, I didn't encourage him." Lyra clenched her fists, digging her nails into her palms. "He knew how things worked in this business, so I'm pretty sure all he wanted was to piggyback on my fame."

"And that made you angry?" Denton pressed.

"I'm used to people treating me that way, and I like to give deserving people a helping hand. What annoyed me were his incessant calls, sense of entitlement, and that kiss."

"Angry enough to make him stop calling permanently?"

Lyra gasped, and Cinnamon growled.

George, who'd lingered by the door until now, entered the room with no apology. "If you're going to continue in this way, I think Ms. St. Claire should have the opportunity to call her lawyer."

Officer Denton hesitated for a heartbeat, eyeing the beagle warily. "We have all we need for now. Please don't leave the city, as we may have further questions."

He marched out, and Officer Shaw shot her an apologetic look before following.

"Can you believe it, George? They think I killed a man because he kissed me."

"I heard, but if they really did, you wouldn't be sitting here. You'd be down at the station."

BEAGLES LOVE CUPCAKE CRIMES

She flinched at the idea of being in a cell. "Then why did they make it sound that way?"

"It's a game to scare you into confessing, just in case you did do it."

"I can't say I care for that game."

He shrugged. "It is a bit old-school, but I guess it might still occasionally work."

"You don't believe I did it, do you, George?"

He raised an eyebrow. "I'm not going to dignify that with an answer. You need to get home and then out to the airport."

She regretted asking. "Thanks for your support and for reminding me about my guests. I better tell them about this in case the paparazzi get wind of it and turn up here." Her stomach churned at the prospect.

Why were these things happening, and were they connected in some way?

## 19

M aggie stayed back at the apartment, checking that everything was in order. Grateful that she didn't have to deal with this, since her mind was in shambles, Lyra used the ride to the private airport to concentrate on what she would say to her guests.

Dan opened the partition. "Do you think they'll change their minds about staying?"

"I couldn't blame them. There's a murderer on the loose, and Kaden doesn't need any adverse publicity that being around me might generate."

"Didn't George say they couldn't consider you a suspect?"

"Rumors don't live in truth."

He nodded. "Well, you'll know soon enough. The plane just landed. I'll stay here with Cinnamon, but if you need me, just call."

Cinnamon fussed as Lyra went to leave, pawing at her arm, and Dan came to collect her. Her pooch sensed she was troubled, but once she was out of sight, Dan would ply the beagle with treats he thought Lyra knew nothing about.

Sporting her beige look, Lyra's red hair was out of sight,

but as the plane taxied to the large hangar doors, she was still jittery from the last time she was here. She shook her head. Dan wouldn't let her come by herself if he didn't think it safe, and there had been few cars or people anywhere near the place.

Nevertheless, once she was inside where several more private planes were housed, Lyra kept up a continuous sweep of the building and small parking lot where Cinnamon waited with Dan. Apart from the crew from another plane and a lone security guard, the place was quiet.

The sound of an engine drew her attention, and a few minutes later, her plane taxied up and stopped a few feet outside the hangar. When the door opened, Kaden was the first out. Even from where she stood, he was easy to spot. More than six feet, he towered over the pilot and Angie. With his fair hair falling over his forehead, casual clothes, and confident walk, he was easy on the eyes. Butterflies fluttered in her stomach. He would see La Joliesse for the first time, and Lyra wanted him to love her.

They collected their bags and headed her way. Colin, nearly as tall and very distinguished in a navy blazer and dark pants, saw her first and pointed her out to Kaden, who waved. Angie dropped to the rear, walking fast to keep up with the long-legged men as they crossed the concrete floor.

Kaden smiled gently. "Are you okay?"

Her sleepless nights must have been showing. "I could be better," she admitted.

"What's happened?" He frowned. "Did you change your mind about needing us?"

"It's nothing like that." By now several people had arrived for a flight. They'd noticed Lyra and were edging closer. "Let's talk in the car." She led the way out, checking to ensure there were no fans lurking outside. Dan waved to them from across the road.

From beside her, Kaden snorted as they neared the limousine. "Still traveling in style, I see. By the way, that plane is freaking awesome too. Thanks for sending it."

"You're welcome. I wish I liked flying enough to enjoy it."

"Still hate it?"

"Silly, right?"

He shook his head. "Not at all. We all have our phobias."

Dan coughed. "May I take your bag, sir?"

Lyra introduced them. "This is Kaden Hunter, our new chef; Colin Tapper, who's going to give George a hand with the wedding; and Angela Leigh, an expert waitress."

Colin gave a small bow while Angie flushed.

"Temporary chef, maître d', and waitress," Kaden corrected her.

Lyra laughed. "Temporary—of course."

"Hello, girl." Kaden saw Cinnamon through the partially open window and reached in to scratch her head.

The beagle all but bent her body in half, her tail a blur, as she tried to get to him. Not until they were all inside did the beagle settle down, closing her eyes to the belly rubs and head scratching from her new fans.

"It's not a long drive, but would you like a drink or a snack?" Lyra pointed to the small cooler and cabinet.

"We had plenty on the plane," Kaden explained. "Now tell me, what's all this new drama about?"

Lyra frowned as the limo moved out smoothly into traffic. She'd start with Symon. "I just fired my agent."

"Isn't that good? Sounds like he was a bit lax, and you were overdue for a change."

"It is good in so many ways. Only he was with me from the start, and I'm not sure I can continue my career outside the restaurant without him and his contacts."

"Assuming you had valid reasons for letting him go—and from what you've said previously, you did—I don't believe that for one minute. You're so famous, no one's going to care who represents you. *You* are the product they want."

"Product?"

Even Colin looked at Kaden with distaste while Angie was absorbed by the limousine's interior, Cinnamon, and the conversation in equal measure.

Kaden smiled ruefully. "You know what I mean. Who you are matters just as much as what you do."

Lyra raised an eyebrow. "As I see it, that's the problem. Everybody wants me to be something I'm not."

"You only have to be who you are—a wonderful chef who is kind and generous. You help so many charities because you believe in them, which in turn encourages others to help. That's the real beauty of your position, and none of it could possibly disappear overnight."

"You sound like Maggie giving me a pep talk." She brushed off the compliments. "How do you know about the charity work? Was it Maggie who told you?"

He grinned. "Maggie is clearly a great asset, but did you think I wouldn't follow your career and try the recipes you're famous for? Think about it. I'm just one of your fans who owns a restaurant and genuinely likes you. You're our very own Nigella, and everyone loves her."

Lyra blushed, having heard the reference since the early days of her career. A reference she couldn't object to since, along with the hair coloring, they had a similar build and, above all, a passion for food. "I don't think about that," she said honestly. "My focus has always been on the home cooking side of things."

Kaden snorted. "You have a famous restaurant, which hardly serves up home cooking."

She put a hand up in surrender. "Okay, the restaurant is important, but the cooking shows are another thing altogether."

"You show that passion every time you cook, no matter where it is. You have fans that hang on your every word and chefs doing the same. They'll be knocking on your door again once the dust settles."

Lyra gulped. "Your faith in my abilities only highlights that I've been a terrible friend."

Colin looked out the window while Angela gaped at her admission.

Kaden laughed. "Yet here I am, despite you having no clue that Phoenix was my restaurant."

Heat hit her cheeks once more. It really was unforgivable, even though the twinkle in his eyes proved he was teasing her. She took a deep breath. "That being the case, it's extremely good of you to return the favor and help me out."

Kaden sat back and shrugged. "Let's not pretend that working at La Joliesse isn't going to give this poor chef a little kudos that might work in my favor to get Phoenix back on the map when she reopens."

Lyra nodded, understanding that it could help him, and not believing for one minute that was the true reason he was here.

"Where are we staying, Ms. St .Claire?" Angie asked shyly. "Not that any hotel name will mean much, when I've never been to LA before."

"Call me Lyra, and I'm taking you to my hotel apartment suite."

Kaden frowned. "All of us?"

"Just you and Colin. I hope that's okay?"

"It must be big."

Lyra was confused. "There's two bedrooms."

"We're sharing?" He looked at Colin, and not in a good way.

Lyra laughed. She really hadn't explained things properly. "I'm going to stay with my assistant, Maggie. Her apartment's on the same floor as mine, and Angie will also have a room down the hall. You two will have your own rooms."

Colin shifted awkwardly in his seat. "We couldn't impose by kicking you out of your home."

"It's no imposition, and Maggie is fine with having a roomie for a few days. We often share suites when we travel. Sometimes even the same rooms when there's been a mix-up."

This was true. It was actually a nice change to spend the evening relaxing with Maggie because she'd missed out on a lot of girlfriend time. Her life could get lonely when she was traveling or stuck in a strange hotel for days. Going out was harder in places that knew her well, and often she wouldn't leave her room except for whatever she was hired to do—a show, signing, or book launches. An apartment simply worked better than a hotel room. But both were susceptible to intruders.

She took a deep breath. "Actually, I have more news. My rooms were broken into recently. All the locks have been changed, but I thought you should know."

"Don't worry about us. Colin has a great rapport in dealing with intruders." Kaden winked.

Colin nodded. "I was in the army, and I'm pretty adept at hand-to-hand stuff. Like your driver."

Lyra gaped. "How did you know about Dan?"

"We served in the same regiment. I recognized him immediately. Good guy," Colin added matter-of-factly.

She caught his eyes through the open partition, and when Dan shrugged, she nodded. "He certainly is, and it's a small world. However, I don't think any of those particular talents will be required. We'll drop you off so you can get settled. Then, when you feel up to it, Dan will bring you down to the restaurant to have a look around."

"The flight was only a couple hours," Kaden protested.

"I'm happy to go with you after you drop off Colin and Angie."

Colin groaned. "Are you crazy, Chef? I'm dying to see La Joliesse for myself."

"Me too," Angie said shyly. "If that's okay."

Lyra laughed, pleased that they were so eager. "Dan, change of plans. The restaurant, please."

"Yes, ma'am."

As the limo turned at the next set of lights, Lyra gently asked, "Any luck with the adjusters?"

Kaden nodded. "Actually, they arrived after I sent you the first text. It's going to be a long process, but the bones of the restaurant are fine, and I have my insurance policy. It's making the restoration happen quickly that will be the trying thing. Coordinating contractors, as you know, is a nightmare. Thank goodness Phoenix didn't burn down completely. Half the kitchen could function as it is, but there's smoke damage everywhere. How or why anyone did it is beyond me."

"I'm sure the police will find that out. I have to admit that the whole business was a wake-up call. I'm getting Dan to look around and check that we've got enough safety measures and security in place."

Kaden nodded. "I'm sincerely glad something good might come out of it."

This was the Kaden she knew. Even hurting the way he must be, he was still generous. She looked out the window and grinned. "Here's my other love!"

Cinnamon, paws up on the window ledge, barked in recognition as the limousine pulled up in front of La Joliesse. Lyra tried to see it for the first time as the others might. The glass frontage was tinted in a way that allowed all occupants to see out clearly, but people looking in could barely see faint shadows, even with the lights on.

Dan waited by her open door, while Kaden and Colin were already out and staring up at the sign. It was rather large, and no one could ever say her restaurant was hard to find. Angie climbed out and stood beside them.

"Wow!" Kaden said, followed by a whistle.

"That's it?" she teased.

He grinned. "Double wow. Since we lost all the glass, I might steal some ideas for my frontage."

"Feel free. It's the strongest available, and I love the feeling of openness yet privacy."

"I need to get inside," Colin said.

She laughed, loving their reactions. "This way."

It was midafternoon. Lunch was over, with dinner preparations beginning as soon as they cleaned the kitchen. George had the front door unlocked before she could find her keys. Bless him, he understood how Lyra would want them to enter this way to get the best impression.

She went in ahead of them and turned in time to see their expressions. Seeing how the layout affected new customers never got old, and Kaden's opinion mattered more than anyone's. Not only did he understand how a first impression could affect the whole dining experience, but the two of them had bounced ideas off each other for years and even sketched a few.

La Joliesse was a product of those discussions, and his look told her he remembered. Arms wide, he turned in a circle.

"It's amazing and nearly exactly the way you said your restaurant would look."

Lyra stood beside him, following his gaze. A long bar took up the right-hand side of the room. The kitchen was on the other side of the back wall, which had two double doors close to the middle of it. The building was on a corner site, and the windows at the front carried around to the left side and led to the covered patio area outside. This had a vibrant hedge in wooden planters to separate it from the footpath as well as drop-down curtains should the weather require them. Hanging baskets were positioned above the hedge, and, aided by sunlight, color suffused the area.

Colin and Angie oohed and aahed as they carried on into her state-of-the-art kitchen, which glistened. Kaden checked out every station with a practiced eye the way she'd done at Phoenix. Overhead, pots hanging from hooks gleamed. She chewed a nail, waiting for him to say something. Anything.

Finally, she couldn't contain herself. "Well?"

He faced her, his eyes crinkling at the edges. "Surely you know how great this place is. I've never seen anything like it, and I've worked in some fancy restaurants. You've not only thought about the customer but about the staff as well. Everyone has room to do what they need, and you have every gadget and device all chefs desire."

"It's stunning, even in here, which is not my domain at all." Colin grinned as he opened the walk-in cooler. "This is massive."

Kaden nodded. "You've created a thing of beauty. I always knew you were a great chef, and a great chef needs a great kitchen. It's perfect, and so is the restaurant."

"Check out the pantry," she boasted, opening large barn doors that slid into internal cavities.

He gasped. "You could get another restaurant in here."

She laughed. "Not quite, but it can store so much that we buy all the nonperishable items in bulk. It saves a heck of a lot of time for my head chef and his assistants."

He nodded thoughtfully. "And money, I imagine. You've made some wonderful additions to what you said a restaurant should have. Perhaps, since you saw Phoenix before the fire, you could help me design a better interior?"

"I'd love to, even though Phoenix was great how she was.

I found the interior to be one of my biggest challenges but one I'd happily repeat."

Kaden grinned. "It'll be like old times working on plans." Then he frowned. "I know how busy you are, so don't think you have to spend time on it if you can't."

"Let me worry about that." She tilted her head. "Besides, I might have more time very soon."

He snorted. "If you're talking about the lack of other work, don't give it a thought. You'll have people chasing you with or without an agent. Like I said, you have your own connections now."

"Thanks, I needed to hear that again. To be honest, the relief of not having to worry about what Symon might put me up for next, or if he'll leave me to the mercy of the press, outweighs any worries about not getting more shows or having contracts renewed tenfold."

"The more I hear about this guy, the luckier he is that he's not anywhere I can see him." He clapped his hands together. "Now that we've got that sorted, surely it's time for coffee?"

Lyra slapped her forehead. "What a terrible host. I haven't even asked you if you want anything to drink or eat, and here we are in a restaurant."

"Not just any restaurant, but coffee will do for now. I imagine we have things to go through concerning this secret wedding?"

"I'll make the coffee while you two get started," Angie offered.

"Are you sure?" Lyra asked. The poor girl had been ignored while they inspected the place, but Kaden was right, there were a lot of things to go over.

"I was a great barista before Kaden hired me," Angie admitted.

Lyra admired her confidence. "In that case, you'll be far better at it than I will ever be."

"Hah! A chef who can't make coffee," Kaden teased.

"I swear that thing does not like me."

Angie grinned and went to check out the fancy yet evil machine, and Colin headed back out to the restaurant.

Kaden stopped when he was just inside her office. "Even this room is magic."

"Magic is exactly how I feel about La Joliesse, and I want that to be reflected in this wedding." Pulling her diary toward her, she then fired up the laptop and twin screens. "It might look like overkill, but I need to visualize everything to know how or if things will work."

He moved a chair to sit beside her. "Just like a recipe," he acknowledged. "I've studied the menu on your website, and the pictures are amazing. Your reviews are mostly 5 stars, and nothing below a 4.7. I hear La Joliesse is full every day you're open, so you already know what will work for a large group."

"We don't often get cancellations and have a waitlist every night," she admitted.

"The media get some things wrong, but the way they talk about you and La Joliesse has to be spot-on. You're famous for the way you cook, and I bet your chefs are almost as good to maintain that kudos."

Pink-cheeked, she picked up a folder. "My head chef is amazing. We don't like to disappoint, and we fit people in if we can, but I never overcrowd the way I'll have to with this celebrity wedding. It's a big deal, and you know how the press can turn in an instant. With everything that's happened, including the hurry to bring it forward, I'm worried I'm overlooking something."

"I'm sure you've got it under control." Kaden turned his attention to the menu. "You're expecting a hundred people?"

"It's going to be a squeeze, but I've said yes. Please tell me I'm not crazy."

He nudged her gently with his shoulder. "I'm not here to humor you, so we'll just have to make it work. The doors from the restaurant open to the patio area, right?"

She nodded and pulled up a picture of the restaurant layout. "They slide back into their own cavity, so they don't take up any room. There's just a small step down."

"Good. That area seats how many?"

For the next hour, they went over scenarios, and Kaden, a spectacularly good artist, made a new floor plan on a blank sheet of paper. He asked great questions and, even better, helped her answer them.

She ran a finger over the configurations. "The only issue is the place settings. They have a seating plan, which won't work with the extra twenty people."

Kaden snorted. "I think they'll be a little more lenient given what they're asking. Let's get this copied and sent to the bride. She can make adjustments on her end to save time."

Lyra hoped he was right. Movie stars were a different breed altogether when it came to what they wanted and what they'd accept. "Maggie will be here soon. She'll contact them and get the names of the additional guests so we can make up the place cards."

"You do them here?"

Lyra enjoyed his astonishment and proudly showed off another gadget.

"See that machine over there? We do a lot of weddings, and there are always issues. Celebrities change their minds all the time. So, they come here, choose a design, and Maggie gives them three samples. Once they've decided, she prints the cards. It means we can update place cards at the last minute if necessary."

He whistled. "You've thought of everything. Right, let's see the menu."

"My favorite part."

Before they'd finished, Maggie arrived, and Lyra spent a little time going over what she needed her to do.

"By the way, here is the list of properties I think might suit you." Maggie dropped a folder on the desk, her eyes twinkling. "You might not have time right now, so bring them with you when you come home. I'll take Cinnamon with me and give her another walk."

Lyra returned the knowing look with a glare. Maggie was matchmaking, which was silly. She loved Kaden, but it was no more than just as a friend.

# 20

When the staff arrived and got to work on preparations for the dinner crowd, it meant the kitchen became a great deal noisier. Used to the hubbub, Lyra and Kaden worked methodically until a knock at the door interrupted them.

Lyra beckoned the man inside. "Kaden Hunter, meet my head chef, James Anders. I'd be lost without him."

The men sized each other up before shaking hands.

"I've read about you," Kaden said. "According to the articles, you were an up-and-coming chef in your own right before you came here."

"Working with the best in the business seemed like a no-brainer to me, and I've never regretted a minute in this kitchen. Lyra says your food is amazing. I hope ours will be just as impressive to you."

James's English accent was charming, and the young chef's humility seemed to impress Kaden.

"James has proved his worth over and over, and that's why he has total control of La Joliesse's kitchen when I'm away. He's also produced his own signature dish and was instrumental in La Joliesse getting her first Michelin star."

Kaden raised an eyebrow. "No wonder Lyra's so proud of you. I look forward to seeing you in action."

The admiration the two men showed each other didn't hide their competitive natures. Lyra looked forward to them going head-to-head; the restaurant could only win from it.

"Lyra, do you have time to look at the menu samples for today?" James asked nonchalantly.

"Absolutely. Facts and figures are necessary but can't compare with being in the kitchen taste testing. How about you, Kaden? Care to check them out?"

He gave her a side-eye. "What do you think?"

James gave a half bow. "First course is on the left, mains down the middle, and dessert on the far side."

Every chef, no matter the level of experience, loved to have their plates tasted and commented on. Naturally a compliment was ideal, but the best of them wanted to know if the dish could be improved.

"A little more seasoning will lift it," she told Belinda, who'd made a salad and, more importantly, the dressing.

James nodded, and so did Kaden. As they went around all the stations, they discussed each dish, and she was delighted with their suggestions and the way they offered them.

"You've got a great team," Kaden said when they'd finished sampling. "The suggestions were small, and they took them willingly. I have no doubt that if it's as good as what you serve every day, the food will be a hit at the wedding. Thanks, Chef. Now I should check on my staff."

Lyra raised an eyebrow. "Our staff, I believe. George will have talked to Colin by now. I explained everything to my staff earlier, and they'll show them the ropes, so there's no need to worry about him or Angie."

"You mean they're learning how to do things your way?" he teased.

She winked. "It is my restaurant."

"Yes, Chef. I just hope you don't steal either of them. Seriously though, thanks for letting Angie come. She won't have anything to do for quite some time with Phoenix closed, so this is a great boost to her morale."

"About Angie—I had an idea. She told Maggie how much she wanted to be a chef but can't afford to train anywhere except on the job. We both know how tough it was to raise the money to get into chef school and then afford to stay there. I like her determination and confidence, and, bearing in mind your directive about stealing her, with your permission, I'd like to offer her free training here until you're up and running again. I'm happy to keep the rent paid on the room she's staying in for as long as she's here, and I'll pay her a decent wage."

Kaden's eyes bugged out. "That's huge. Are you sure?"

"If we can help each other as well as others with potential, then we should."

He smiled. "I'm sure she'll be delighted, and I'm happy for her to train with the best."

"Enough with the compliments." She laughed. "If you're sure you don't mind, I'll ask her as soon as I can, unless you want to."

He shook his head. "It will mean more coming from you."

Although he seemed genuinely pleased for Angie, Lyra got the impression that something else was troubling him as he watched the hive of activity in the kitchen. Although, he was probably thinking about Phoenix which must be depressing.

"Do you want a hand with tonight's menu?" he suddenly asked.

"We have a full team, and you must be tired. I didn't mean to keep you so long. Do you want to head over to the apartment? Dan will be happy to come get you."

He looked disappointed. "Are you going home or staying here?"

"I'm going to poke my head in the restaurant and say hi to the staff and then a few customers when we open. After that, I thought I'd go back to Maggie's apartment and see how she's doing. Now that Symon's not around, things are a bit of a mess with my schedule. Plus, she's been looking for a new apartment."

"She doesn't like the hotel?"

Lyra slapped her forehead. "Good grief, I've never asked her that. She's actually looking for me. With all the trouble and other residents being bothered, I can't stay there much longer."

"All the trouble?" He frowned. "More than one incident, then?"

She grimaced. "I don't want to discuss it here. Let's talk about it back at the hotel. Meanwhile, you can wait for me here or keep looking around. The choice is yours."

"Hah! For a chef there's no choice."

He laughed, but she could tell he wanted details. Maybe fresh eyes on her continuing problems would help.

When they were ready to leave, Lyra and Kaden found Dan waiting in her office.

"Sorry to keep you waiting." Lyra eyed the empty plate in front of him.

"I'm not. James thought I looked hungry." Dan rubbed his stomach in satisfaction. "Working for you has its perks, and that guy sure can cook."

"He is pretty good." She laughed. "And you deserve plenty of perks with all the overtime you've put in lately."

"You know I don't mind, and I have a confession. I've done something without asking you. It's been on my mind for some time."

Lyra raised an eyebrow, and beside her, Kaden stiffened. Since Dan always had her best interests at heart, she wasn't worried by his admission. "I'm listening."

"I've brought my car to take you home. It's no limousine, but we should be able to get the five of us in there." Dan wiped his face on a napkin. "Going forward, I think we need something less conspicuous for day-to-day travel."

"I've been saying that for a long time," she reminded him gently.

"I know, but Symon wouldn't budge on it." He stood and walked to the door. "A limousine is great when you're going to an event and want people to notice you. Everyone knowing when you come or go from the restaurant, or your apartment, is asking for trouble. It doesn't take an Einstein to figure out who's inside and what your routine is."

Kaden helped Lyra into her coat. "That makes a lot of sense. The more I hear about this Symon, the more he sounds like a complete jerk."

Still embarrassed by her lack of strength in challenging Symon's directives, Lyra had to agree. "I don't need a limo at all and wish I'd done something about it sooner. Changing cars could have saved me so much anguish over the last few years."

Kaden squeezed her shoulder. "The important thing is you're doing something now."

She nodded. "And there must be plenty of other changes I can do to make this career of mine less painful."

"Painful?" Kaden asked. "Why would you want to do something that makes you feel that way at all?"

They were following Dan to the back door where Angie and Colin waited, and Lyra spoke over her shoulder. "That is a very good question. Let me get back to you when I can think of a good answer."

The black car had tinted windows. Lyra had never seen it before and wondered if Dan bought it specifically to keep her safe. While it was a sweet thing to do, she didn't want him to be out of pocket. She would speak to him when they were alone.

When he pulled up at her hotel, she said, "Take a break, Dan. We'll see you later."

He nodded, and since he'd also called ahead to the hotel, they used the secret entrance again. The service elevator wasn't as fancy, but it was great not to worry about other residents getting in and bombarding her with questions.

They entered Lyra's apartment as a group. Maggie stood at the dining table, which was covered in brochures. "Hi, everyone. I hope you like the rooms."

"What's all this?" Lyra pointed at the table.

"Some more properties I think you'll be interested in. There's not as much room in my apartment to lay them all out, but I can pack them up if you haven't the time to look at them now."

"Don't hurry on our account." Kaden stalled them from gathering up the papers. "We have nothing to do tonight, so we aren't going to kick you out of your home."

"I didn't look at the others yet, so it makes sense to study them together. If you're sure you don't mind?" Lyra asked.

"Not at all. We can unpack and keep out of your way." Kaden looked around him. "Where are our bags?"

"Dan already dropped them off. You'll find them in the rooms down the hall. There's a bathroom in between, which I'm afraid you'll have to share."

The men followed her pointed finger, and Lyra turned to the women. "Angie, would you like to see your apartment?"

"A whole apartment for me?"

"It's not the size of this, but it's comfortable and has a separate bedroom."

Angie grinned. "I have a studio in Portland, so the addition of a bedroom sounds palatial."

"I'll take her." Maggie nodded at the table. "You've got a bit of research to do."

Lyra sighed as their chatter and laughter trailed behind them. She took a seat at the table. It looked like it would be a long evening.

Cinnamon wandered around the apartment, nosing at bedroom doors while Lyra flicked through a few of the brochures.

"I bet you're confused, sweetie. Things will be a little different for a few days, but I'm sure you won't mind the extra company, and you like Maggie's place."

"Anyone would think she was a person the way you talk to her."

Kaden's voice made her jump, and then she laughed at the truth behind his words.

"She's sweet and clever, which makes her almost a person. Plus, she's great company, and we've never had a cross word. Would you like coffee?" She was already on her way to the kitchen.

"Unlike you and me," he said wryly. "Let me make it."

Lyra dropped a pod into the machine. "You're my guest, and thankfully this thing makes the darn stuff on its own."

He smiled and took a seat at the counter. "So, what other problems are you having?"

Her hand stilled at the cupboard. "You remembered."

"I'm like an elephant. And it sounded important."

Taking out two mugs, she placed them by the coffee machine spluttering into life. "I wanted to tell you right away, but I know it will bring us both down. You were at the competition in Portland, right?"

"Briefly. Why?"

"Did you happen to see the awards and who the winner was?"

"Not live, but it was on TV later." Kaden frowned. "The winner kissed you."

Lyra was relieved he'd seen it for what it was and not that she'd wanted or instigated that kiss. "That's right, and now he's dead."

He stared for several seconds. "I'd make a joke about that, but you're serious, aren't you?"

"The police dropped by earlier today to tell me and give me the third degree."

"No way." He gasped. "They thought you had something to do with his death? Were you even in Portland when he died?"

"That's just it. He died the day after the contest ended."

His eyes widened. "When you were helping me with the wedding?"

Out of her bag, Lyra pulled the clippings from the paper and displayed them on the counter. The silence grew heavier as he studied all three pictures.

"Kid's got some nerve," he growled over the first one. "Anyone can see you weren't encouraging him to kiss you. I have to admit that it's not a bad one of us, and I'd like a copy. However, the one with your agent in the park speaks volumes about your relationship."

Lyra shivered. "Maggie and I think Symon instigated this article. What bothers me is that you might be implicated in some way."

"If the police thought that, and since the death occurred in Portland, they would have visited me by now."

"Maybe they hadn't connected us before you left. It certainly took them a while to get around to me."

He shrugged. "I'll deal with it if they do."

"I hope you don't get any flak from this."

"Lyra, we've done nothing wrong. You of all people should know you just have to weather the storm of the press. There's little you can do to stop them unless they accuse you of something bad enough to warrant a fight."

Lyra worried her bottom lip with her teeth. "There's something else you need to know. I wanted to tell you earlier and all your team before you unpacked in case you'd rather not stay here."

Kaden frowned. "Why wouldn't we?"

"During that break-in a few days ago, I was asleep, and Cinnamon didn't hear a thing. Nothing appeared to be touched except for my laptop, which was smashed."

He stiffened. "You weren't hurt?"

"No, but whoever it was, they knew the door code. Like I said, the codes have been changed, so you should be safe, but just say if you'd prefer to go somewhere else, okay?"

He shook his head. "I don't have much with me that anyone would want to steal, so I'm not worried."

She frowned. "Are you sure? It's just that there have been so many incidents and now another death."

His eyes widened. "I read about that girl in Boise. Wasn't it suicide?"

"I don't believe it was, but the police couldn't find any leads to say otherwise. Maybe they're not related, but don't you think it's too coincidental?"

"I'm not a big believer in coincidence. You've done all the right things by alerting the police, staying with Maggie, and changing cars. As long as you're not alone, I think you'll be safe."

She knew he was right, but she still couldn't shake the feeling that something else was going to happen.

Something as bad if not worse.

## 21

The next few days went by in a blur. Having her best friend at her side for more hours than she could have hoped for made each day a pleasure. Kaden had a few suggestions to streamline the menu to save time, and they spent many hours trying them out. Eventually, they made decisions that would work efficiently given space, time, and dietary stipulations.

Ingredients were ordered. Cutlery and plates counted. Glasses sparkled, and centerpieces would arrive soon, as well as fresh flowers for the entranceway. Decorations hung inside, and the "private party" signs were ready to go up outside so would-be diners would refrain from trying their luck for a table.

Kaden also suggested hiring background screens painted to look like a garden. They would cover the drop-down sides and give the patio privacy in case the paparazzi got wind of what was happening. It was a masterpiece and added to the spring theme of the wedding.

Lyra walked through the restaurant, checking everything with Maggie, and then they did the same to the kitchen. With no lunch service, due to the Monday closure, they were able to put all their focus on the event.

The hustle and bustle gave Lyra an adrenaline rush, and when she saw Kaden, who was in charge of the salmon starter, she could tell he was in the same zone. Resplendent in his whites, he looked as though he belonged at La Joliesse.

"All under control, Chef?" she asked.

"Yes, Chef. I believe everything's going according to plan."

For confirmation, they looked to James. With an unspoken signal, three pairs of eyes swept the kitchen, and then they nodded at each other.

"All staff arrived early and have worked solidly," James stated seriously. "We're on schedule. Lisa also came in to help with the napkins, and I said she could come back to watch, as long as she didn't get in the way. I hope that was okay."

Lyra grinned. "It's fine, and great that everyone's pitching in. What do you want me to do first?"

"The dessert station needs some help. If you have time?" he suggested a little awkwardly.

"There is always time to ensure perfection, isn't there, Kaden?" she teased, delighted when he laughed at the inside joke, which had been one of their trainer's sayings at cooking school.

Although adept at any course, desserts were Lyra's forte. Plus, it freed up her dessert chef to continue with other tasks.

First, she baked the profiteroles, which were tiny choux balls sometimes called cream puffs. They didn't take long, but she needed three batches to make the triangle-shaped pyramid called *le grande croquembouche*. Beating the ingredients to make the choux pastry made her arms ache, but the silky smoothness gave her a sense of satisfaction. This would be a good batch.

After cooling, she made a small hole in each with a

skewer she used for this purpose. Next, she piped dulce de lita into a third of them. The next third had a filling of ganache, and the last was more dulce de lita with the addition of limoncello.

Now came the hardest task. Dipping each one into the sugary toffee, she patiently laced them together. Once assembled, she drizzled a little melted chocolate from top to bottom and finally added another drizzle of more toffee.

"That's amazing!"

Angie startled her, and Lyra noticed she had an audience. So engrossed in making the pyramid perfect, she'd been unaware of anyone else in the room.

James gave her a small bow. "You've outdone yourself."

"It's perfect. Not the slightest tilt." Kaden circled the workstation. "Did you use a cone?"

Cones were standard and made the pyramid more stable, but Lyra shook her head. "I've made them many times, and I like the fact that everything is edible."

Kaden took another walk around it. "I'm in awe. And you made the wedding cake as well. Can we take a look?"

Lyra led them to the table where the cake was hidden under a large cover. Despite worrying that she wouldn't have time, Lyra assisted in making the three-tiered wedding cake yesterday. It would be talked about nearly as much as the whole wedding, and anything but favorable reviews for La Joliesse wasn't acceptable. Assembled and decorated, Lyra sighed happily as she lifted the cloth.

Maggie arrived just then, and with a hand to her throat, she exclaimed, "Oh, Lyra, that is the most beautiful cake ever."

Lyra took a step back and smiled happily. "Hopefully our couple will think so too. Especially the bride."

Suki Love was a perfectionist, and if things had gone as planned, her wedding would have been far more lavish than

Lyra and her team could provide on such short notice. But Lyra couldn't deny that the cake looked classy.

"How could she not love it?" Kaden said. "It's a work of art."

"Then it will be worth all the last-minute rush." Lyra turned away to hide the blush from his praise. Coming from him it meant a great deal. "The guests will be arriving soon. Shall we get changed into fresh whites?"

"Definitely." He followed her into her office where she kept her uniforms.

"Let me get you one of James's. Mine might fall off you, and the front won't fit quite right." Lyra's curves needed a much different style than the average chef's outfit, and it had been a source of amusement to Kaden when they were at school, where one style was used for everyone. This meant she had to get a bigger size so it didn't gape at her chest but hung off her everywhere else. Once she got the TV show, hers were custom made. The difference would be blatantly obvious to him, as his grin suggested.

"Actually, I brought my own. It's a better fit that way," he teased.

She rolled her eyes, enjoying the banter.

Once they were changed and freshened up, it was time for the doors to open to early guests—of which there were many. Suki and Heath had their own security, but because she trusted him implicitly, Lyra had Dan working the door. He diligently checked names off the clipboard Maggie had organized.

They would be needed back in the kitchen soon, but there was a little time to be available for the bridal party if they wanted her, and James had everything under control until then.

Glamorous wasn't a word that did the guests justice. As far as Lyra could tell, clothing made by the leading fashion houses was worn by almost every woman, and most of the men had suits from Armani. Maggie made hasty notes for future reference.

Beside her, Lyra and Kaden watched discreetly in a corner by the bar—until a guest arrived who had the ability to make Lyra ignore her own rules of keeping a low profile at events like this.

Those rules kept her safe from upstaging anyone. It wasn't about her on these occasions, and she hated any distraction by zealous fans. However, this was an exception she was prepared to make without guilt. Or, at least, very little.

Raine Riley, who she had met once before, stood in the middle of the room surrounded by women, some of whom Lyra had met, many whom she recognized. A fashionista who catered for the more curvaceous woman, Raine dressed in a way that Lyra admired and often chose to emulate. Now wasn't the time, but she would love to meet her again if the opportunity arose.

"Maggie, please let me know when Ms. Riley is leaving."

She spoke softly so Kaden didn't hear, and her assistant smiled knowingly.

"If you hadn't asked, I would have spoken to her myself and teed up a meeting. That woman knows her stuff. Isn't she gorgeous?"

"She truly is." Lyra sighed wistfully.

Maggie picked up two baskets and whisked by Lyra to hand out paper cones of rose petals—an idea she'd stolen from Kaden's bag of tricks, with his permission.

"You have nothing to be envious of." Kaden nudged her shoulder.

She laughed softly. She should have known he wouldn't miss the exchange, and she nudged him back. "I've missed my best friend constantly talking me up."

"That's what friends do. Doesn't make it less true."

Lyra would have said something flippant, but the wedding was about to begin. The wedding planner, Suki's lead suspect in releasing information to the press, had been kept out of the loop, so Colin and George greeted everyone, and with the help of Angie and other staff members who took coats, they showed them to their seats. Now they encouraged the guests to stand along the aisle to welcome the bride.

Suki was dressed in something that might have been made by Raine. The dress, dripping in bling, hugged the movie star's stunning figure in a way Lyra admired, and was only outshone by the sweet smile Suki bestowed on the room. She held on to her father's arm until they reached the patio area, where she was handed to her groom, who had waited patiently when informed that his wife-to-be would be twenty minutes late.

The two bridesmaids stood to one side, as did the groomsmen. The mother of the bride stepped forward to hand Cutiepie's ruby-and-diamond-studded lead to her daughter, then moved back to the front row. Cinnamon watched from the corner of the patio, her tail wagging furiously at seeing Cutiepie again.

With all the doors open, everyone could see the ceremony without too much difficulty. Initially, this had troubled her when Kaden suggested having the ceremony out here. He was proven right again. The flow was much better this way. She heard murmurs from the guests about the oddity of having the ceremony at a restaurant, but she really thought it worked. Suki appeared delighted with the setting they had created, and even better, the paparazzi had thankfully yet to make an appearance.

The guests pushed closer, and to her delight, Raine Riley came to stand beside her. Lyra tamped down a nervous giggle. It would be unprofessional to go gaga over a guest, but Lyra was awestruck, and that wasn't easy to hold back. She'd felt this way about a few chefs she'd wanted to emulate and then later met as an equal. She figured she'd done okay with the fangirling, but a fashion designer was different. And not just any designer. Raine was an icon for all plus-sized women who liked to dress well yet comfortably.

Out of the corner of her eye, she saw Maggie and knew her assistant would be cheering her on to make contact. In fact, Lyra could guarantee that Maggie intended to push things along if Lyra chickened out. She was being silly. Raine wasn't exactly a stranger.

"Good to see you again. I love Suki's dress. Did you make it?" Lyra whispered, pleased she sounded normal.

Raine nodded. "I did. It's a little fussy for my taste, but the bride had set ideas. What can you do?" She gave Lyra a conspiratorial wink.

Raine was a little taller than Lyra's five-eight, her hair of a similar length, only wavier and darker. She had gorgeous cheekbones, but it was her eyes that were the most compelling. A sea green, they danced with laughter at her joke.

"What indeed?" Lyra grinned. "Wait until you see the cake."

Raine turned back to Lyra. "I bet it's spectacular. I watch your show all the time, and I'd love to get a peek up close."

Lyra's grin wouldn't quit. "Would after dinner and before dessert be a good time? Otherwise, I'll be cooking, and I'd like to show you myself."

"That's so kind."

"I admit that I have an ulterior motive. With all the appearances I do, I need new clothes constantly. Your clothes. Any chance you could make something for me?" There, she'd said it, and now Lyra held her breath.

"I'd love to, but I know things don't always go as planned. If we don't catch up tonight, give me a call, and we'll work something out." Raine took a card from her small bag, which was shaped as a replica of her dress: red with silver chains and hearts.

Lyra was about to reply as she took the card, but the celebrant began the ceremony. She stood quietly beside Raine as the couple said their vows, and both women sighed when the groom wiped a tear from his eye while professing his love, and again when they were pronounced husband and wife and kissed.

Lyra was a little misty and wasn't the only one. Even Raine sniffed delicately into a lace-edged handkerchief beside her.

A cheer went around the room, and the flash of a camera close by distracted her. Petals now draped the guests and tables as well as the couple, who were besieged by well-wishers. When she looked back, Raine was gone.

The arch was quickly removed and an area set up for the photos that utilized the garden backdrop. Emilia Corban, the photographer Lyra had recommended to Suki and who was fortunately available on short notice, snapped away at the bridal party in her pleasant way, making it run a lot smoother than it looked.

It was time to get back to the kitchen, but someone called her name.

Emilia scrambled between guests to get to her. "It's so nice to see you again, and I know you're busy, but could I take a picture or two of you for the bride and groom's magazine article? It's an exclusive."

Lyra was taken by surprise by the petite woman's request. "I don't think your readers will want to see me."

Emilia tucked her fair hair behind one shoulder and blinked. "On the contrary. Where this wedding took place will definitely sell copies. It's the whole package—two movie stars, a secret wedding, plus a celebrity chef."

"Sounds like a romance novel." Lyra grinned. "But I'm not convinced. Are you sure they want me included?"

The photographer nodded. "I've got a list of photos Suki wants, and you're on it as well as Cinnamon." She pulled the paper from her pocket and handed it to Lyra. "Did you know that the payment for the article will be sent to the couple's charity, which is animal welfare?"

Lyra didn't need to think about it any longer. She'd long been a supporter of that particular charity, as were Emilia and Raine, so it was not only appropriate, but Lyra would also do pretty much anything to help the cause.

"In that case, just give me a minute to get all the chefs who helped make this work." Lyra hurried to the kitchen, but from the corner of her eye, she thought she saw someone who shouldn't be here.

Her breath caught. *He wouldn't dare... would he?*

Although she scanned the room several times, she came up empty. Darned if she wasn't imagining things.

## 22

K aden was checking the soup when Lyra burst through the door. He dropped the spoon he used for tasting and met her in the middle of the room. "What's happened?"

"Nothing horrible," she assured him. "We're needed for a photo. Can I drag you away for a minute or two?"

"What? Why? This is your promo opportunity, not mine. Surely James should go with you?"

James shook his head and glared from nearby, making Lyra grin.

"James doesn't like to leave the kitchen until the end of the cook." She gave Kaden the megawatt smile she was famous for. "Trust me. It's important."

"It better be," he said in his best growly voice.

Lyra merely laughed, then stopped by her office to collect Cinnamon, who'd been left there by Maggie, and took them through to the patio from the door off the side entrance. Emilia was at their side in a flash and sat them at the table where the couple had signed the registry. Placing the bride's bouquet in front of them, she snapped several pictures.

"Smile, you two. I promise it won't be too painful," Emilia teased.

Kaden rolled his eyes, and Lyra nudged him.

"The quicker you get with the program, Chef, the quicker you can get back to the kitchen."

He looked down at her, and his face softened. "You owe me."

"More than I can repay." She smiled up at him. "But I aim to try."

"That's perfect," Emilia murmured her pleasure as she clicked away. "Look at me. Now at the flowers. Nice. All done."

"Tell me again why we're in the photos?" Kaden asked.

"Suki wanted pictures of anyone who played a part in making today work." Emilia smiled. "Some of them will be sold or used to promote animal welfare. Can we get Cinnamon and Cutiepie on the chairs, please?"

Lyra picked Cinnamon up and placed her on the chair that Emilia indicated, while Suki's mother stood beside them holding Cutiepie and looking pointedly at where Kaden sat.

He got up quickly and had to steady the chair as it began to topple.

"It's a great cause, and I hope the pictures help," Lyra said.

"I'll send you copies once it's published, if you like?" Emilia called as she snapped away.

Lyra was delighted by the offer. "Yes, please."

Emilia nodded but was already organizing the next group, so Lyra gathered Cinnamon and moved out of the way. Some people might be unsure what to make of the chefs in their whites when everyone else was so colorful, but seeing them receive preferential treatment in the photo shoot encouraged several guests to follow them.

Lyra expected a certain amount of that at one of her weddings but wasn't prepared for Rosetta Larkin. The Bgrade actress pushed past Lyra and threw her arms around Kaden's neck, causing him to stumble.

"Hello, handsome! I had no idea you'd be here today."

"Likewise, Rosie. How are you?"

"Still missing you, baby. And now you're a star too." She spoke in a purr, and once she'd released him from the hug, she linked her arm through his.

"It's always nice to be missed, but I'm hardly a star." He gently pried her fingers loose.

She laughed loudly. "Don't be so modest. You've done so well with that restaurant in Portland."

Kaden frowned but didn't enlighten Rosetta about Phoenix's fire. Besides, the woman was already focusing on her next target.

"Have you seen all the famous people in this room? I simply must talk to that photographer. I hear she's the one to look out for at the moment." Rosetta was about to move on when she deigned to notice Lyra and leaned down from her stilettoed height. "Don't I know you?"

"Surely you've heard of Lyra St. Claire. *The* Lyra St. Claire," Kaden said proudly.

A glint lit the actress's eyes. "Oh yes, the chubby cook who owns this restaurant."

"Rosetta!"

Lyra shook her head at the poor acting. Rosetta knew exactly who Lyra was, because she was the kind who made it her place to know everyone who mattered, and not just in LA. "It's okay, Kaden, I've heard worse. Although, not usually as blatant."

"Bit sensitive, isn't she?" Rosetta sniffed.

Kaden glared, keeping his voice low. "Why do you do that? Lyra doesn't deserve your meanness."

"Whoa. Could the great coolness of Kaden Hunter be melting at last?"

"Lyra and I are very good friends and have been for years. I look out for my friends, as you should know."

Under his glare, Rosetta shifted uncomfortably. "You're right. I don't know her. Maybe she is nice."

He gave her a withering look. "Some people are."

A touch of sadness infiltrated Rosetta's hard facade. "There aren't too many like you, Kaden, so don't go thinking there are." She wagged a finger in Lyra's face. "And you better treat him right."

Lyra stood her ground. This was her restaurant, and no one could undermine that.

Kaden stepped in between them. "We're needed back in the kitchen. I'm sure you can find someone who'd be only too happy to talk to a movie star, Rosie."

"I daresay." The actress nodded, already scouting the room. "Wowza! Do you see who's over there with the bride's family? I didn't see Mr. Gorgeous come in, did you?"

Rosetta sashayed across the room, pushing herself between a good-looking actor and the bride's father, who was a star in his own right and didn't take kindly to the interruption. If she had any awareness at all, she'd know that by the look on his face, but Rosetta clearly didn't have that going for her.

Kaden shook his head. "Sorry about that."

"Hey, you didn't make her insult me, and I've seen her in action before today. So, you and Rosetta are close?" It was surprise that made her ask.

"I happened to witness her violent breakup, which you probably read about."

Lyra nodded. "It was in all the papers."

"She provoked him, but that's no excuse for what he did. I took care of her when she had no one. Although she'd like people to believe otherwise, it wasn't a relationship."

That made more sense. "She was lucky to have you around."

He shrugged. "I could hardly leave her in the state she was in. I just wish she learned something from that night, but she seems bent on self-destruction. Come on, the kitchen is where I'd rather be."

Despite Kaden's explanation, Rosetta had left a bad feeling in the air. The press could get things so wrong, and people like Rosetta fed into the lies and innuendo with no thought for whom they hurt.

Lyra pushed through the swing door into a world where she was much happier.

## 23

---

Adding the final touches to the first course, Lyra nodded to George, who waited by the kitchen door. He signaled to the line of waiters, including Angie, who stood along the far wall. In a practiced motion, they picked up three plates of salmon each and filed out the other door, followed by more waiters carrying baskets of hot rolls.

It was a great feeling to begin service and even better having Kaden by her side. The time flew by, and soon they were cleaning up so they could lay out the plates for mains.

That moment of sheer happiness faded when a face she didn't want to see, the one she'd put down to imagination, peered around the waiters and, at the first opportunity, darted between them. He came forward with a little hesitation, as if trying to gauge his reception. Her glare couldn't possibly be deemed encouraging, but that didn't stop Symon.

He stared at Kaden as if he couldn't believe his eyes, then focused on her. "Lyra, it's so good to see you."

It took all her willpower not to yell at him to get out. "Symon, what are you doing here? As you can see, we're really busy."

"I must insist on a minute of your time. It's very important. We could go into your office?"

She glanced at the door. *Where is security?* With no intention of stopping work or being alone with him in her office, she looked pointedly at the large clock on the front wall. "Very well. You can talk here, but only for a minute."

Symon side-eyed Kaden. "I see you're managing just fine."

He couldn't have started the conversation in a worse way. "As I'm sure you know, no one's banging down my door to have me on their shows right now, and *A Lesson with Lyra* is on an extended hiatus due to the last tabloid feature. However, the restaurant is doing well. Thanks for asking." She rarely employed sarcasm and doubted Symon would understand that was what it was.

Kaden apparently did and made a point of laying out plates rather noisily.

Symon frowned and came closer to Lyra. "The cancellations were due to happen without a firm agent, but that's not why I'm here. This wedding was a bit of a surprise. I believe it wasn't scheduled for a couple months. Lucky you had it to fall back on, thanks to me."

Lyra stiffened. "What do you mean? Luck had nothing to do with it. I made La Joliesse successful using my skills, not yours, and that attracts important events."

"Easy to say now, but it was the other work that made you famous first. This restaurant and anything else you do are by-products." He scoffed.

Clearly nothing had changed, and there would be no apology for his actions. "We'll have to disagree on that, and you were paid well for your efforts."

"What I did for you was worth more than money," Symon insisted.

Kaden moved in front of her and placed both hands on the counter to lean toward Symon.

"Surely the work came about because Lyra's a fantastic cook and people love to watch her doing just that."

Symon grimaced. "I wouldn't expect you to understand how fame works. I guess you have plenty of time right now to work for Lyra, unless it's more of a personal visit."

Kaden looked ready to jump the counter. "You mean I have time because my restaurant nearly burned to the ground?" he growled.

Symon snorted. "That's an exaggeration. I heard it's mainly smoke damage."

He didn't jump the counter; instead, Kaden circled it.

The agent's eyes bugged, and Lyra debated with herself whether to intervene. *Why couldn't he just leave?*

Now on the same side of the counter, Kaden looked ready to wring information from Symon—literally.

"Do you know something about the fire? Like how it started?" Kaden asked through clenched teeth.

Symon backed away, tripping in his haste. He grabbed hold of the counter to save his fall, his face a mottled red.

"Don't be ridiculous. I don't know you, and I've never been to your restaurant."

"Never been near it or never been inside?"

"N-N-Neither."

It sounded like Kaden believed Symon was involved, and Lyra's skin prickled. It was possible. Knowing about the fire wasn't the oddest thing—it was the way he described the incident.

Symon always seemed to have information that others didn't, but how could he know those details unless he'd spoken to the fire department? Surely they wouldn't reveal anything relevant to the investigation to anyone other than adjusters or the police. Did he have contacts within those departments? These thoughts stretched her imagination, despite knowing Symon had dealings with people from all walks of life.

From conversations she'd overheard, Lyra had suspected for a long time that Symon had shady dealings. Ones that were worse than bribing people to get what he wanted, which he didn't hide. But there could be more of that kind of thing which he wasn't as overt about.

There'd been a couple 0f incidents when she'd seen him talking to Duane Buchanan. While that wasn't a crime, he knew how Lyra felt about the man, and she'd asked him to stop giving him work and telling him about their plans. If only she'd challenged him more when he'd denied and brushed off her concerns, lost his patience, or seemed greedy.

However, none of that explained how Symon could orchestrate the fire or why he disliked Kaden so much.

But this wasn't the time for these questions, and they'd been distracted enough. She wanted Symon out of her kitchen and to get through the rest of the night without another incident.

"Kaden, we don't have time to get into this now. Symon, you need to leave. In case you hadn't noticed, there's a wedding to take care of."

Symon stood straighter, looking less scared now that Kaden had backed off. "Did I forget to mention that I'm a guest?"

Lyra gritted her teeth for a moment. If she was a violent person, his superior look was incentive enough to give in to the strong urge to wipe it off his face. "I didn't see your name on the list?"

"I was a last-minute addition. I'm with Rosetta Larkin," he said smugly.

Kaden snorted. "Congratulations?"

"It's not like that. We're friends," Symon stated, staring at Lyra as if that should be important to her.

The tension between the two men was palpable, and there were underlying nuances from both of them that Lyra couldn't grasp. "How did the two of you get invites?"

Symon shrugged. "Rosetta was coming with someone else, and they couldn't make it, so she asked me."

"Are you her manager?" Lyra asked.

He smirked. "That's a possibility for the future, but right now I'm just her plus-one."

"You better not be here to cause trouble," Lyra warned him.

"Why would I do that? I was fired despite doing my best for you. Tonight, I wanted to check on how you're doing—because we're still friends."

His voice dripped with false sincerity, and she didn't bother to correct him about the friendship angle. "I'm glad you're moving on. I wish you all the best and hope you enjoy the wedding."

"Being here with Rosetta, I'm sure it will be amazing. She's a party girl from way back." He winked at Kaden, then sauntered out the swing door.

"All right, the show's over. Let's get the next course out," James called across the room.

Getting everyone back on track took precedence, but Lyra wouldn't be able to forget that Symon was out there.

# 24

Symon's interruption caused them to run a little behind schedule, and it took a while for Lyra to get back into the rhythm of her work.

Feedback was perfect for the first course, and as the last of the mains left the kitchen, Lyra gave a large sigh and looked around the room to where the rest of the staff took a quick breather between courses.

James nodded from across the aisle, and they shared a smile of recognition for a job well done. It was time for dessert, and, as with the last two courses, one hundred plates leaving at as close to the same time as possible took careful coordination. Lyra watched over the proceedings, unable to relax until the last plate of food was served. Then she walked around the entire kitchen, stopping to thank each staff member and compliment their contribution.

With coffee and petit fours being served by the waiters and cleanup nearly finished, Kaden's job was done.

Unbuttoning his whites, he removed his hat. "Well done, Chef."

"Well done yourselves, Chef Hunter and Chef Anders.

Now that our guests are fed, how about a coffee? Or can I interest you in something stronger?"

James gave a sheepish grin. "If you don't mind, I have a late date."

"Of course not. I'll see you tomorrow. Kaden, what about you?"

"I think a quiet drink would be a perfect way to end the day, if you have time?"

"I have a few minutes before I check on things. George will let me know if there's an issue."

Lyra led the way into her office and opened a small cabinet. Taking a bottle of red wine from her cupboard, she poured them a glass each. Twirling hers, she gave him a rueful smile.

"I don't normally drink until the place is empty, but I think we deserve it."

"We definitely do. That was full-on. I can honestly say I haven't worked that hard since Phoenix first opened. How about a toast?" he suggested.

"Anything in particular?"

She touched her glass to his, recognizing the matching adrenaline rush in his eyes and restless hands. It was always this way after a major service and took a while to calm down from the high of so much pressure and giving your all. Especially when you knew you'd done your best.

He raised his glass. "To a job well done and happiness for the marriage."

"I'll drink to that." Lyra sighed. "Let's hope it lasts."

Kaden frowned. "You were never so pessimistic before."

She shrugged. "Being around celebrities does make you a little jaded about love. The way they jump into a relationship, believing they've found their soul mate without really knowing each other. Then they find out the truth—that they were never a match—and five minutes later, they call it quits."

He took a sip of wine. "It saddens me that you've let all the negativity you've seen affect you."

Since Lyra considered herself an optimist, she was stunned. It troubled her that she hadn't been aware of a change of heart.

"I guess leaving Fairview and then Portland has a lot to do with it." She twirled her glass again. "I know love does exist. I'm just not sure it can last in cities like this. It would have to be a special couple who could wrangle all the ups and downs of life in the spotlight." Lyra laughed. "Don't mind me, I'm just tired. You're leaving tomorrow, aren't you?"

Kaden frowned. "I wish I could stay longer, but Colin and I have a mountain of things to do."

She put her drink down and sighed heavily. "I understand. This was fun, and while I don't wish Phoenix any more drama, I really hope one day we can work together again."

There was a slight pause. "I had an idea about that."

Lyra leaned forward eagerly. "I'm intrigued."

"Since you aren't doing those shows, which I imagine you'd scheduled in that diary of yours, you might have some spare time. In which case you could come and do some appearances at Phoenix."

The words hung in the air while she wondered if it was a possibility.

His expression changed from hopeful to horrified. "Did I come across too needy? I would pay your going rate, and while it would help certainly help get Phoenix back on her feet, it's also a way to cook together again. It was a sugges-tion, that's all and believe me there's no pressure to say yes."

She put her hand up to stop him from further embarrass-ment. "It's a very good suggestion. I think I can make that work, and I'd hoped you would ask me to the reopening of Phoenix."

He breathed a sigh. "Thank goodness you didn't take it the wrong way. I have a terrible foot-in-mouth problem, which is why I usually let Colin handle any negotiations."

Lyra laughed. "Luckily I understand how much you suck at it."

They both sat back and grinned. The years apart were fading.

Lyra checked her watch. Although weary, she felt obliged to stay to ensure nothing else was required from the most prestigious wedding held so far at La Joliesse. "Do you want to come to the restaurant? I'd like to see the bride and groom as they leave."

"Sure." Kaden raised an eyebrow. "The thumping music does imply that they're having a good time."

She groaned. "As you know, that's not the same thing at all." Like Kaden, Lyra preferred to run her restaurant with a calm ambience rather than have loud noise as the backdrop, but events like these were too lucrative to pass up.

"True. I guess after that I should head back to the hotel to pack." He stretched. "If I don't fall asleep first."

"I've organized Dan to collect you and Colin late tomorrow morning and take you to the same airport."

"It's certainly a fantastic way to travel," he admitted. "By the way, thanks again for having Angie train here. She's so excited and adores you."

"That's sweet. She slotted in so easily and is a quick learner. I have no qualms about how well she'll do."

Lyra took a moment to slip a shirt over her undershirt and touch up her lipstick while Kaden donned the dark blue shirt he'd arrived in.

It was going to be hard to say goodbye.

## 25

They were just in time to see the bride throw her bouquet. Suki blew her a kiss as they ran down the aisle lined with their guests and mouthed a thank you. Lyra waved enthusiastically, glad it had all worked out. They looked so happy, and she truly hoped Kaden was right about these two.

When the doors closed behind the happy couple and the dancing resumed, she turned to thank him again. Unfortunately, Symon chose that moment to butt in.

"Well, look at you two, all cozied up," he slurred as he staggered toward them.

"Symon, you're drunk," she stated the obvious while looking around to find something to divert him from further conversation. Nothing came to mind.

"It's a wedding, so I'm sure I'm not alone. Besides, I needed a party to help me feel better about being ditched by my favorite client who never appreciated me."

Several guests edged closer. There was nothing like a bit of scandal to grab people's attention. Lyra knew there was no point in arguing with a drunk in general and, from experience, knew Symon could become aggressive, so she decided to ignore him. However, when she made to walk past him, he grabbed her arm.

"You were nothing before I met you," he sneered.

The ugliness of his words and anger sickened her. How had she stood his bullying for so long? She looked pointedly down at his fingers digging into her skin and, taking their audience into account, said calmly, "As a matter of fact, I had a TV show first. Then you were hired. Now take your hands off me."

Whether it was her words or that she hadn't backed down, he grew angrier. "The show didn't make you famous. I did that!"

Lyra looked around for security. Most had gone with Heath and Suki, but over the heads of the remaining guests, she saw Dan doing his best to get from the front door to her. He wasn't finding it easy.

"You heard her. Let go now," Kaden growled, towering over the red-eyed agent.

"Or what?" Symon taunted.

Kaden's blue eyes darkened as he took a step closer, their faces now inches apart. "Don't tempt me, or I'll show you."

Symon dropped her arm like a hotcake and backed away. "You're both going to be very sorry for this."

Kaden followed, with George, Colin, and Dan arriving to back him up. "Get out of this restaurant. Under your own steam—or mine."

The four of them maneuvered Symon to the door one step at a time while Lyra followed, smiling at the guests so they weren't alarmed, but he chose to make another stand.

"I was invited. You can't kick me out."

Kaden held the door open. "I'm sure the bride and groom have no idea who you are. Plus, the restaurant reserves the right to ask a guest to leave if they're inebriated, which you certainly are."

"You have no authority, and Lyra's not asking," he said stubbornly.

This was taking too long, so Lyra pushed between Colin and George. "I'm done asking. I'm telling you to leave right now." She was firmer than she'd ever been, which didn't make him less angry, but he moved.

Symon glared at each of them before he walked through the doorway and headed down the street. They followed, watching for a short while to make sure he wasn't coming back.

"That wasn't pleasant." Lyra's voice was ragged. "I'm sorry for his rudeness and grateful you were here to help."

George shook his head. "No need to feel sorry. We were keeping an eye on him, but the man was drinking everything not nailed down and moving around a lot. I'd be happy if we never see him again."

Lyra shivered.

"You're cold. Let's get inside." Kaden led her back to her office, where Cinnamon jumped around her until she pulled the dog into her arms. "I'll stay until you're ready to go home."

"After Symon's performance, I'm ready now."

"Good. I think everyone else is here to have a good time, and the boys will ensure it stays that way until they close up."

"Hopefully you're right. I hate confrontation, but I'd feel bad if they had to deal with another moment like that, no matter that it was overdue." Lyra was a little annoyed with herself for continuing to shake. It was that awful look in Symon's eyes that had her so upset. She didn't choose to end things on a bitter note, but now she saw that anything else had never been possible.

Kaden merely nodded. "Wait in here while I check if Dan's ready."

Lyra rubbed Cinnamon's back, which calmed them both. A determination slowly rose inside her. From now on, she would make sure Symon had no hold over her. And since she had more money than she could ever need, there was no reason to do everything that came her way. If she could spend her time cooking, here or at Phoenix, instead of traveling for weeks at a time, that would be a better life.

Without her shows, what would she lose? She'd miss the contestants but not everything else that went with it. Like feeling responsible for every contestant who didn't win or wasn't treated fairly. Instead, she could train people like Angie and give them a leg up into this highly competitive world while steering them away from the many pitfalls.

A smile grew as she pictured how that would look.

Collecting her bag and Cinnamon, Lyra was near the patio door when her daydream was shattered by the screech of car tires. Several fast heartbeats later, it was followed by a loud bang and the crunch of metal, which reverberated around the restaurant. Then more screeching tires.

By the time she put Cinnamon back in the office and reached the front door, the guests lined every window, necks craning and several deep. Pushing past those at the door, Lyra felt the chill of the night air, smelled exhaust fumes and the stench of rubber. Colin was several feet to her left, bent over a body.

Fear had a grip on her long before she knew for sure it was Kaden.

## 26

C olin knelt beside him. "Are you okay, boss?"

Kaden groaned. "I'm fine. A bit sore from where I hit the wall."

"I'll call an ambulance," Lyra croaked from his other side, already punching buttons on her phone. "And the police."

"I don't need an ambulance."

"Did he actually hit you?" George arrived out of breath and immediately checked Kaden's limbs.

Kaden tried to sit up and winced. "Just a nudge."

"On purpose?" Colin growled.

"I can't say for sure, but it seemed pretty deliberate when he veered toward me."

"Not stopping is bad either way," George snarled. "I chased the car to the next corner, but it was already gone. I think I have the plate details though."

"Good work. I'd rather wait for the police inside, and you need to write the details down before you forget."

Lyra touched his arm. "You shouldn't move until you've been seen by a paramedic."

He squeezed her fingers. "This pavement isn't exactly comfortable, and I'm okay—really."

Frustrated by his insistence, Lyra could do no more than watch while he struggled to his feet with the men's help. She led the way and pulled out a chair for him at the first table, but he shook his head with a grimace.

"Thanks, but I'd be happier in your office, if that's okay?"

She nodded, trying to keep the horror from her face. Limping his way across the restaurant, his lips pursed, and his forehead was damp with sweat. In the brighter light, she saw that his right eye was swollen. In fact, it was nearly closed.

"What on earth happened to you, Chef?" Angie yelled from across the kitchen, dropping cutlery on the counter to rush to his side.

Kaden sat down with a groan in the closest chair inside the office. "A small brush with a car is all."

"You were run over?" Angie asked incredulously.

"Nearly." Kaden closed his eyes. "I was lucky."

"Is the driver okay?" she pressed.

"I'm assuming so. He took off before I could ask."

Angie gasped. "A hit-and-run? Do you know who it was?"

"Right this minute, a headache of lethal proportions has taken up residence inside my skull, so a little quiet would be appreciated," Kaden snapped.

"Sorry, Chef." Angie's face pinched, and her eyes welled.

Immediately, Kaden was contrite. "I'm sorry. I shouldn't take this out on you."

Lyra put her arm around Angie's hunched shoulders. "Would you mind organizing a cold compress as well as a heat pack? George will show you where they are."

George smiled encouragingly, and with a worried look at Kaden, he left with the sniffing Angie.

"I'll make sure the guests are okay," Colin said softly.

Lyra poured a glass of water and put it on the table beside Kaden. He had to be in some serious pain to lash out that way, and she remained silent while they waited.

Kaden drank the water, then sat with his head in his hands. Eventually, he took a deep breath and sat back. "Well, that's one way to end the evening I never considered."

"I guess it's not over yet," Lyra reminded him. "The police will come as soon as they have a car free, but who knows how long that will take?"

He flinched. "You were already exhausted. Go home. The guys will look after me."

"That's not happening." Lyra tutted. "We're in this together."

"This has nothing to do with you."

"I don't believe that, and if you're honest, neither do you."

It took a moment or two before he frowned. "So, you think whoever torched my restaurant followed me here?"

Lyra's stomach clenched. "No I don't. I think all these terrible things are related, and the person doing this wants to hurt me through you."

"But we've only just met up again."

"Precisely. I already had stuff going on, and someone doesn't want you to help me deal with it. I'm protected most of the time and you aren't. Don't you think it's logical that you're the easiest target as a way to get at me?"

"I'm not sure. You have other people close to you. Why go after me?" He winced and rubbed his temples.

"I could be way off base. I probably am. The only thing you have to worry about is getting better." The white around his mouth was enough to have Lyra shut the conversation down. She would share her theory with the police.

Just then the others returned. Angie handed him an ice pack as well as a heat pad, while George placed a bowl of warm water on the table. Colin brought in disinfectant, a cloth, and a towel.

"It's going to hurt like anything, but your hand is a mess, and you don't want to get an infection." Lyra added a few drops of disinfectant to the water.

Bits of stone and brick had punctured his skin, and droplets of blood speckled his clothes. With a deep sigh, Kaden slowly immersed his hand while chewing on his inner cheek.

"Any sign of the police, George?" Lyra asked.

The maître d' moved away from the door. "I'll get back out there and check, as well as get the CCTV tape. Unless the car was stolen, they should be able to locate the driver through that or others in the area. One good thing about LA is that there's practically a camera on every corner," he added with false cheer.

Lyra touched Kaden gently on the arm. "They'll catch the person and find out if there was something else behind it."

He sighed again. "It was surreal. I heard a car behind me. At first it was just a purr. Then the engine revved. I turned and was blinded by headlights. Thinking it was Dan, I didn't panic, but then it was right in front of me, and my instincts took over. I dove and landed up against the brick building. The bumper caught my hip as I went down. In that split second before I fell, I saw the driver, but most of his face was hidden behind a scarf. I swear he made a beeline toward me."

Lyra saw his confusion as her brain tried to unravel what had happened and what might have led to this moment, because something had to connect this to her troubles. It was clear to her that this was more than a series of unfortunate events. Kaden could have been killed.

George returned and laid the tape on the table. "No sign yet. It's lucky we have an eyewitness," he told them.

"What?" Lyra let out an embarrassing squawk. "This is the first I've heard about that."

"Sorry, I thought Colin told you. It's Dan. He was bringing the car around to the front when it happened. Now he's standing guard, just in case," George explained.

Just then Dan banged through the doors. Looking anxious, he was followed by a man with a medical bag.

"This is Dr. Killian," Dan said through tight lips. "He's one of the guests at the wedding, and someone else said the doctor had his bag in the car. He's been drinking and was reluctant to help, but the paramedics are taking their sweet time, so I thought it would be quicker."

Lyra took charge. "Thanks, Dan. Dr. Killian, this is Kaden Hunter. As you probably know, he's the victim of a hit-and-run."

"I heard." The doctor nodded and, after a thorough check, agreed with Kaden's prognosis. "There doesn't appear to be anything broken. Most of the pain will be due to severe bruising and will take some time to heal, so you should take it easy for a few days."

"Then I can fly home to Portland tomorrow?"

The doctor frowned. "If the paramedics agree, and as long as you make sure to get a checkup and X-rays as soon as you land if you feel any worse, I see no reason why not. What you need is a good deal of rest and no heavy lifting."

"Thank you. I can do that."

Lyra wasn't convinced the doctor was reliable, but as soon as Dr. Killian had gone, Kaden rounded on Dan. "You know who did this?"

Dan's face grew dark. "It was Symon Reeves, and I saw the whole thing. He deliberately tried to run you down."

Lyra gasped. "Symon? Even after the way he's treated me, I can't believe he'd do this."

"I can," George muttered.

"Watching it was like a nightmare in slow motion." Dan's voice shook with anger. "Thank goodness Kaden's got good reflexes."

"But are you absolutely sure it was Symon if it happened so fast, and if he was wearing a scarf as Kaden said?"

"I'm not mistaken," Dan said firmly. "I was parked down the street facing this way, ready for when you needed me. I won't forget the crazy look in his eyes. Besides, the car was a blue sedan, and I recognized his number plate."

Lyra slumped into a chair. "But why?"

Kaden stared at her as if she were crazy.

Maggie had arrived in time to hear Dan's story, and now she snorted. "Jealousy. Symon thought he had the gig as your agent for life. He isn't capable of changing how he works and treats people. I bet he thought you'd see the error of your ways after you stopped getting guest spots and *A Lesson with Lyra* was put on hiatus."

Lyra shook her head. "I made it very clear we were done."

Maggie gave her a pitying look. "There are rumors that you were getting back together."

"You never told me that." Lyra clasped her hands in her lap.

Maggie put a hand on her shoulder. "Because I knew it wasn't true and that it would only upset you the way it's doing now."

"I don't really know him, but I've followed your career nearly as closely as Kaden's, and any photo of the two of you shows him looking at you as if he owned you," Colin added.

"He's been obsessed with you for as long as I've known him," George agreed. "The man isn't fit to shine your shoes."

Dan nodded. "Then tonight, when he might have thought he had an opportunity to make you jealous with Rosetta, it turned sour. Obviously he didn't know Kaden was coming to help you, and I saw the shock and anger on his face when he found out. He dislikes Kaden intensely."

Kaden scratched his head carefully with a bandaged hand. "I don't really understand why. Today was the first time we've ever spoken."

"Don't you?" Maggie asked, her eyebrows skyward. "Since you came back into Lyra's life, she's changed her plans several times and been involved in a wedding that made the headlines without his permission or involvement. He got no kudos for it, and Symon does not like to be thwarted. Then Lyra fired him, and you turned up at her restaurant."

Lyra watched Kaden's outrage turn to sorrow.

"Maybe he would have backed off if I hadn't come back on the scene, and you'd still have your shows."

She didn't want him to feel responsible, but he had that stubborn look on his face. She could be stubborn too. "Don't you dare blame yourself for any of this. Would it be better for me to still be tied to him? No way. After this, the police will catch Symon. Apart from you being injured, isn't that a better scenario?"

Kaden gave a half-smile, which would have to do.

Lyra now had to deal with the fact that not only was Symon responsible for hurting her friend, but he also had an unhealthy attachment to her, which resulted in this hatred for Kaden.

Was Symon capable of murder? A mere few weeks ago, she would have said no, but now....

## 27

Dan took Maggie and Cinnamon home and arrived back at the same time as George, who'd been checking on the last of the guests.

"The police are here," George said.

Kaden sat straighter, but the white lines around his mouth had deepened.

"They'll be coming through in a minute after they tell the remaining guests not to leave until they've been questioned," George explained. "I offered brandy to those who felt like they needed a bit of soothing, and that's keeping most of them happy."

She smiled slightly at the way George had things under control and was thankful once more that the bride and groom hadn't witnessed any of this drama. "I appreciate everyone's support and help."

"Dealing with customers is our job, and while this is unusual, Angie, Colin, and I will handle things like we normally do, so don't worry about us." George nodded at the door. "Here they are now."

Two policemen entered with Dan following. One took

Dan into the back of the kitchen while the other asked the rest to leave so he could speak to Lyra and Kaden in her office.

He asked a multitude of questions in a seasoned manner, and she felt reassured when he mentioned that more CCTV footage would be in their hands in a few hours.

"While there are witnesses to the actual accident, we also want to know how the suspect was behaving. It will take a bit of time to question the guests, I'm afraid," the officer said apologetically.

"That's fine. Take as long as you need. Although, I am worried that Symon will be driving around and could hurt someone else." Lyra frowned. "When he left, it never occurred to me that he would drive because he was so drunk."

The policeman folded his notebook and tucked it into his shirt pocket. "Thanks to your staff member's quick thinking, the license plate number has been dispatched to all cars in the area. We'll catch him if he's still out there." He turned to Kaden. "It would be good if you could stay one more day, Mr. Hunter."

"I'd like to help out, but like I told you, I didn't see who was behind the wheel, and I need to get home to Portland as soon as possible. I'd be available anytime via phone to talk to the police, or I can go into the station there."

The policeman wasn't overly impressed, but he nodded. "Very well. We'll be in touch when we locate the driver."

"Absolutely. Anything I can do to help, just call me."

As soon as the officer left, Kaden turned back to Lyra. "Forget what I just said. If you need me to stay, I will."

She shook her head. "I'd rather you went to the hospital."

"I'm not much for hospitals, but I did say when I get home, I'll seek medical advice if things worsen. Plus, I really do have to get back to Portland. There are papers to sign for the insurance so the repairs can get underway."

Lyra stopped herself from begging. As much as she wanted him to stay, he'd already done so much, and what if Symon tried to hurt him again before he was caught? She couldn't bear the thought, especially as this was mostly her fault for burying her head in the sand.

"I understand. You get back to your restaurant and sort everything so I can come visit and work with you again. Maggie, Dan, and George will be here for me." She pointed to the rip in his jeans and the blood on his shirt. "And the next time we meet, I'll buy you a new outfit."

His lips curved. "No matter what forces want to keep us apart, I want you to know that I'm never going to give up on our friendship again."

"I don't want either of us to do that. Let's get out of here," she said as they walked through to the restaurant.

All the drama, which might have at first been exciting for the guests, had paled now that the music was off and they'd given their details to the police. Even the inebriated had by this stage sobered up somewhat and were drifting off in cabs and limousines.

Lyra said goodbye to George and the staff who were staying on to finish the cleanup in preparation for another full day in the restaurant tomorrow. Dan was at the bar nursing an orange juice while Angie collected glasses with the other waiters. As soon as he saw them, Dan was at their side.

"Can you take us home now?" she asked him.

"I'm ready when you are. Do you need any help?" he asked Kaden.

"I'm fine, thanks. Sorry it's been such a late night for you."

"It's my job to get you home safely, and I'm the one who's

sorry for messing up. I shouldn't have waited in the car," Dan insisted.

"No one expects you to be standing at the door," Kaden protested. "Besides, if you had, then he might have hit all of us."

"But if I had—"

"Enough, Dan. Let's get home," Lyra said, a little choked up by these two sticking up for each other when neither had done anything wrong. "Colin and Angie, you come too so Dan can get on home afterward."

"You'll be glad to have me out of your hair tomorrow," Kaden told her as they walked to the car.

"You know that's not true. No one made this happen except Symon. Understood?"

He nodded, giving Lyra a quick smile, but like the others, his eyes scanned the area.

Kaden sat beside her, a few beads of sweat dotting his brow and upper lip, and he held his arms against his ribs. He'd made out that his injuries weren't bad, but the bruises on his arms and face were already starting to come out. She imagined that he was going to look a heck of a lot worse tomorrow, and the nagging guilt that this happened when he was doing her a favor left a sour taste in her mouth.

"Remember there's absolutely no need to rush off in the morning. Leave only if you feel rested enough. Dan will let the pilot know when you're ready, and he'll take you to the airport."

"That's really kind of you both," Kaden said with sincerity.

"No problem. You deserve to take things a little easy after what just happened," Dan assured him through the partition.

She saw them smile at each other, and Lyra shook her head. *Men!* It seemed they had bonded over a near death and now they were best buddies.

When they got to the apartments and up to their floor, Colin walked Angie to her room down the hall, and Kaden let himself into Lyra's place. Cinnamon rushed past him to make sure Lyra was coming.

"We'll be back here tomorrow night, girl," she said to the confused beagle.

"It's a lovely place, and I'm sure you'll be pleased to be in your own space once again," Kaden said. "Did you want to come in for a drink?"

She shook her head as Colin came toward them. "It's been a long night. I'm sure we could all benefit from some sleep. Will I see you in the morning before you go?"

He smiled gently. "I couldn't leave without saying a proper goodbye. I know it's been a difficult time, but try to get some sleep."

"You too. There are painkillers above the fridge if you need them."

Again, he waited until she and Cinnamon were safely inside Maggie's room. She would miss him terribly, and it would be so hard to say goodbye to him tomorrow.

Lyra felt her resolve strengthen.

Tomorrow she intended to make sure she was headed to the life she wanted. To do that, she would ensure that all her friends would be safe in the future.

## 28

The phone jangling beside the bed pulled Lyra from a deep sleep. It had taken so long to nod off that she was reluctant to answer it, but eventually she couldn't stand the noise.

"Hello?" she croaked.

A deep voice rumbled, "Morning, Chef. Do you fancy breakfast with me before I head off? Colin must have taken pity on me while I was asleep and cooked enough for ten people. He's headed out with Maggie, Angie, and Cinnamon to pick up a few trinkets for family in Portland."

She felt disoriented. Waiting to see what they were up to for the day, Cinnamon never left her side in the mornings. For Maggie to take Cin without a fuss meant Lyra must have been almost comatose.

She sat bolt upright. "I didn't hear them leave. How are you feeling today?"

He yawned. "A little stiff but otherwise fine. Are you coming?"

"Can you give me ten minutes?"

"Take as long as you need. I can't go anywhere until Colin

returns. I figure he deserves to see a few sights before he leaves."

He sounded reassuringly okay, but Lyra needed to see for herself. "Make sure the coffee is hot."

A quick shower, minimal makeup, and a floral dress with a nipped-in waist completed her ensemble in record time. She ran down the hall to her apartment, where the door was unlocked. Kaden sat at the dining table surrounded by plates piled high with bacon, eggs, pancakes, and fresh fruit.

"I see what you mean." She laughed. "Who did he think he was feeding?"

He grinned, swallowing a mouthful of something, and stood, handing her a plate. "I'm thinking the whole building. Help yourself."

Lyra was incredibly hungry and loaded her plate ambitiously. She raised an eyebrow when she sat next to him. "With the busy afternoon and evening, it occurs to me that we didn't eat last night."

Kaden snapped his fingers. "I guess that explains all the food. Maybe Colin and the rest of them didn't eat either."

"That's terrible." Lyra groaned. "It's one thing to forget to eat and another not to feed my staff. We were in a restaurant, after all."

Kaden handed her the syrup. "You're being too hard on yourself. Everyone was busy. Then we had the whole Symon drama. Besides, nobody died from one missed meal."

That pragmatic statement put it all into perspective. Kaden could have died last night, and yet here they were surrounded by a feast. "I'll make it up to them. Maybe cook for them next Monday," she suggested, crunching into a piece of crisp bacon with renewed gusto.

"I'd almost come back for that meal. If only I wasn't tied up with reopening my restaurant," he joked, then added more seriously, "I'm hoping everything gets settled quickly."

"Me too." Lyra smiled, understanding how much it meant to him to have Phoenix returned to her former glory.

They ate in companionable silence until Maggie burst through the door followed by the others.

"I'm glad you're both here. Angie and I came across the magazine with a great article about yesterday's wedding."

"Already? How is that possible?" Lyra dropped her fork, hoping nothing was mentioned about the hit-and-run or Symon.

"Emilia Corban must have sent them straight to the editor. I know they sometimes hold the front page if they have a heads-up that something big is happening. I guess Suki's agent had that covered. Take a look." Maggie placed the magazine in front of Lyra.

Suki Love and Heath Carter were on the front looking starry-eyed and incredibly happy. Lyra and Kaden didn't get time for more than a quick glance before Maggie flicked to an inside page and tapped it with her finger. "Looks like you two are just as famous now."

Maggie was overexcited about the article, and as soon as Lyra saw the picture, she understood. Kaden and Lyra's picture filled half the page. Sitting at the small table, they were smiling at each other. The posy in front of them hid much of their hands, giving the impression that they were clasped together.

"Oh" was all she could manage.

Kaden looked back and forth between Lyra and Maggie while Colin and Angie stood back, highly amused.

"What's the matter? This looks good to me. We're smiling, and it's for charity, right? The picture of the two dogs is awesome too."

Maggie snorted at Kaden's confusion. "Firstly, it's a great picture of you two. You look very… cozy together. Which is wonderful exposure for your restaurants, both of which are mentioned in plenty of detail."

"But I'm missing something else?" he asked.

"You look like a couple." Maggie grinned.

Kaden paled, giving Lyra a quick look. "Don't be silly. Everyone knows we're just good friends."

Lyra shook her head as she came out of the daze of seeing Kaden and her looking... what had Maggie said? Cozy? It could certainly give the wrong impression to some.

As if Maggie read her mind, she nodded. "I'm thinking Symon saw how much fun you were having last night and didn't appreciate it. He really doesn't like you. Is it possible this is what made him go crazy?"

"A photo did that?" Kaden asked in disbelief.

Lyra shook her head. "Not the photo, he wouldn't have seen it. It's the posing for the photo he would have taken exception to."

"If he can't have her, then maybe he doesn't want anyone else to—in any capacity," Colin added.

A light went on behind Kaden's eyes. "So, Symon's in love with you."

"No!" Lyra now accepted he was obsessed with her, but she didn't want that to be true.

Kaden raised an eyebrow. "We all know he has feelings for you."

"But love? He has a funny way of showing it," she scoffed.

"Symon's had feelings for you since forever." Maggie sighed. "Some of those feelings he did make known a while back. Remember?"

Lyra was a little shocked by Maggie's revelation until she thought back to all Symon's sweeping statements and innuendos. They rolled over her like the reruns of a bad movie, and she slapped a hand on her forehead.

"He did once declare that he believed we should be

together. When I told him I couldn't see him as a partner except in business, he was upset and a little angry. It didn't last long, but now that I think about it, that was probably the turning point in our relationship."

Maggie nodded. "I'm convinced that's when he began making bad decisions. Like leaving Lyra to fend for herself, saying it was good publicity. Or making her do back-to-back shows on different sides of the country. I wouldn't be surprised if he had something to do with the fire at your restaurant."

Kaden's expression varied from shock and disbelief to thoughtful contemplation. He got up from the table and began to pace. "So, Symon believes Lyra and I are more than friends."

Maggie nodded at him. "There is the fact that you've been staying in her apartment."

"But not together," Lyra stated, her mind in an absolute turmoil. Even if Maggie was clutching at straws, his obvious manipulation was contemptible.

"He wouldn't know that. It would be enough that Kaden's in the space he wants for himself," Maggie insisted.

Colin stepped forward. "I don't know him, but from what I saw, the man has serious issues around needing to be noticed. Having said that, he barely took his eye off the kitchen doors. He was in the front of the crowd when you were having the photos taken, and he wasn't happy about them at all."

"But Kaden and I aren't an item," Lyra protested, wondering how many ways it could be said.

Kaden frowned. "Maybe looking as though we were was enough for him. Especially if he's a little unhinged."

"He's not some crazed fan," Lyra protested weakly, not even sure why she was bothering to argue when evidence was stacking up.

"He's certainly acting like one."

Wide-eyed, Angie nodded in agreement. "He was also incredibly frustrated when he couldn't get some alone time with you. He complained to me and George about your attitude toward him and offered us money to arrange something. Naturally, we refused."

Lyra grimaced. "Maybe I should have. Then this wouldn't have happened." She held her hand up when the others objected. "Okay, I get it. Symon has major issues, and they aren't my fault. Only, I checked, and he wasn't in Portland the night of the fire. In fact, he flew out after things were set up for the competition. Therefore, he couldn't have been involved."

"He didn't have to start it, but he could have orchestrated it," Colin suggested.

Lyra nodded. "Since he did try to knock Kaden down, or worse, I don't know why I doubt him capable of arson. But why try to burn his restaurant down? He didn't see Kaden and me together the way this picture might portray until after the hit-and-run." She snapped her fingers. "But you're right, Mags, he was incredibly angry about me working at Phoenix."

Maggie leaned against the counter. "I think his control over you was slipping, and he didn't like it one bit. Regardless of when Symon left Portland, he was home in plenty of time to handle security and the media."

"But he didn't, and those were his ways of punishing me." Lyra shook her head sadly. "Finding out how he kept Kaden away and seeing how unapologetic he was about that and all the other things, I can see how he thought he had me under his thumb. The truth is, for the longest time, he did."

"You were young and inexperienced," Kaden said gently.

"Maybe, but I'm not anymore. I'm not going to let him get

away with doing any more harm to people around me." Lyra took a deep breath.

Kaden refilled her cup, giving her an apologetic look. "I was hoping to wait until you'd eaten, but you should know that I got a call just before you arrived. The police have Symon in custody. Last night they found him asleep at the wheel outside his apartment, and he was so drunk that they couldn't question him until today. The CCTV footage came through as well and shows him staggering to his car, then driving it at me. There's also a broken front light, and the glass matches what they recovered from the scene."

Lyra sat back, her hand over her eyes. Symon was obviously guilty, no matter that she didn't want it to be true. Any of it. Having him at her side for most of the last four years, she'd never considered him capable of hurting someone unless it was verbally. She didn't approve of that either and told him so, but this was horrifying.

"You should talk to the police again," Maggie told her firmly. "Tell them everything."

Lyra lay her clasped hands on the table. "What can I say that I haven't already when there isn't any proof that he started the fire?"

Kaden touched her shoulder. "Maggie's right. If the CCTV footage was conclusive here, they can do the same at Phoenix providing there are cameras nearby. If they find the person who started the fire, that could lead them back to Symon."

Frustrated, as this was not how Lyra wanted things to end, she had to see things through here and make sense of the past before she could move forward. Needing all the facts and the reasons why something happened was what made her successful. Sure, this wasn't a recipe, but it was her process and the only way she could get closure. To get that, she needed a plan.

She stood, drawing their attention. "Okay. Here's what we'll do. I'll call the police and tell them I'll be there soon. Dan will drop Colin and Kaden at the airport, then take me downtown. Maggie, you should stay with me. Bring your laptop or notebook, and we'll make a list on the way of things that seem relevant to proving Symon's guilt. Angie, there's nothing you can do to help, so please take the day for sightseeing. I'll speak to you later about a plan of action for your time here."

There was a buzz in the room as they jumped into action. Organizing a team was Lyra's forte. Disappointingly, the time she wanted to enjoy with Kaden before he left evaporated. Symon struck again, and he wasn't even around.

Lyra, Angie, and Maggie cleaned up the breakfast mess, then collected their coats. The men met them and Cinnamon at the elevator, and after saying goodbye to Angie, they headed to the airport. As they drove, Lyra murmured to Maggie, who jotted notes on a pad. Focusing on something else made the drive easier.

When the limousine pulled up close to the entrance of the private hangar, Kaden, Colin, and Lyra got out. Dan shouldered Kaden's bag and was heading to the plane when Kaden called out to him.

"No need for that. I can manage."

"You shouldn't be lifting anything heavy. Besides"—Dan winked—"I thought you might like time to say goodbye."

Colin followed Dan with a knowing nod while Maggie stayed in the limousine holding Cinnamon who pressed her nose to the window.

Kaden grinned. "You have a great bunch of employees."

"They're more than that to me. I trust them, and I really like them." She screwed up her nose. "Even if they are all buying into this more-than-friendship thing."

"I'm glad you have them and don't let it get to you." He

shrugged. "You and I had our chance, and what we have is better than any romance."

She nodded. "One day they'll understand that what we do is what we love, and it has to come first. It's taken me a while to get to a point where I can enjoy that again."

"That's good to hear. Did I tell you how glad I am that you fought for this friendship and didn't let me wallow?"

Lyra gulped. "I wish I'd done it sooner."

"I have an idea." He smiled gently. "How about no more regrets? Let's enjoy our careers and spend time together as often as we can."

"You always have the best ideas."

"Clearly not always." Kaden looked down at the colourful bruise on his arm. "But I wouldn't change a thing. I loved working at La Joliesse, and I'm pretty sure the celebrity wedding will keep me on the map until Phoenix is up and running. Thanks, Lyra."

"It's me who should thank you. Without your help, Suki's wedding would have been a worse drama than it was."

He shook his head. "It wasn't a drama until the end of the night. The wedding itself couldn't have gone better."

"That's true." Lyra smiled. "Call me when you get home."

"Sure. Stay safe, and good luck at the station."

She waved, aware that she'd rather be on that plane than visiting the police. Now *that* was weird.

Once he'd boarded the plane, she climbed back into the limo. On the drive, her phone rang. The name and number came up for one of her suppliers, an organic vegetable company that catered to high-end restaurants.

"Tony, this is a surprise."

"Hi, Lyra. Is everything okay?"

She flinched. "Things have been better. Did you hear about the drama last night?"

"Last night? No."

"Never mind. What did you call about?"

"This is a bit awkward." Tony paused. "I'm sure it's an oversight, but your account hasn't been paid. We're still just a small company, and I can't afford to give much leeway. I'm sure there's a logical explanation, and I did try to get Lisa first before bothering you, but she didn't answer."

Instantly Lyra's stomach knotted. "Lisa's usually great at paying on time, so maybe it's a glitch with the bank. I'm so sorry, Tony. I'm out of the office, but leave it with me and I'll get back to you very soon." She didn't mention that she was headed to the police station and hoped it wouldn't take too long. A good relationship with suppliers meant a great deal to her, but more than that, this did not feel right.

"I'd appreciate that. Have a great day."

She heard his relief, and the knots tightened. Her policy was to never pay a bill late. Lisa knew that. And she'd never had an issue with her bank. She turned to her assistant. "Mags, have you heard from Lisa?"

Maggie shook her head. "According to George, she's off sick for a few days with a bad flu."

"That's odd, she looked fine to me at the setup for the wedding. Anyway, she usually sets the payments up for Friday, but if she was sick, maybe she didn't get around to it and forgot to ask someone else to take care of them."

"Is that a problem?"

"Tony hasn't been paid. Now I wonder if he's the only one."

"George would have mentioned it if she'd asked him. He's usually the backup, right?"

Lyra's stomach churned some more and rather than answer she found Lisa's number. She would apologize for disturbing her if the woman really was sick, but she had to know that this was merely an oversight. The call went through, but no one answered.

"I might just check the accounts." With shaking fingers, Lyra tapped the bank app on her phone. Those seconds it took to load, then type in her login details and password were the longest she'd ever known.

"Lisa's wiped me out."

Maggie gasped. "Lisa? You're kidding?"

Lyra handed her the phone. "It could only have been her."

Maggie opened up a transfer of five thousand dollars. "This payment went into Symon's account." Her fingers flew over the screen. "And this! But he had no passwords because you changed them."

"He didn't need them if he had Lisa on his payroll." Lyra took back the phone. "There are a lot of withdrawals, small enough to not arouse suspicion. Wait, this account is different and there's no name attached. I wonder if it's Lisa's."

"So they're in this together." Maggie tapped Lyra's arm. "Don't you have to sign an authority for large withdrawals?"

Lyra shut her eyes and groaned. "A while back, Lisa came to me with papers to sign for new suppliers. I should have studied them closer like I intended, but the whole wedding thing blew up, and I left them on my desk. I never saw them again. When I got around to asking James about them, he assured me we had the same suppliers. It never occurred to me that there was something shady going on, and I assumed James had simply changed his mind about switching."

"Lisa must have used my signature to give her permission." She sucked in a breath not wanting to believe what her mind was telling her. "You don't think James is in on this?"

"James adores you." Maggie sighed heavily. "But what do I know? If Lisa is behind this, even with Symon pulling her strings, then my ability to read people is broken."

The continuing betrayal hurt more than losing the money, and Lyra groaned. "I'm beginning to wonder if I ever had any." Silence hung heavy for a few seconds. "Dan, turn the car around."

With no hesitation, he did as she asked, and Lyra gave him an address. "Hurry, please."

"That's Lisa's address isn't it?" Maggie frowned. "You said she wasn't home."

"I said there was no answer."

Dan glanced at her in the rear mirror. "This is crazy."

"I know, but it certainly looks like Lisa is at the heart of this. Maybe someone coerced her into stealing from me, and while that points to Symon, there must be more to it. Lisa didn't know Justine or Adam as far as I know."

"At least tell the police where we're going," Dan pleaded.

"As soon as we get there. She might be more honest with me."

"I don't like it," he growled. "Don't think I'm not coming in with you."

One look at his narrowed eyes and Lyra knew she couldn't stop him. "Maggie, will you stay with Cinnamon? I'd hate for her to bark and alert Lisa."

Her assistant sighed. "Okay, but if you get hurt, I'll be furious. Either of you."

Dan flashed Maggie an intrigued look in the rearview mirror, and if she'd been in a better frame of mind, Lyra would have laughed.

## 29

The street was tidy except for Lisa's semidetached house. Peeling paint and an overgrown lawn made the place look sad.

Lyra made a quick call to Officer Denton, filling him in before hanging up and putting her phone away. Dan made Lyra walk behind him, and they crept slowly up the path. When they got to the door, Lyra lifted and dropped the shiny brass door knocker in the shape of a unicorn. Footsteps could be heard approaching, and again Dan stepped in front of her.

"Lisa? It's me, Lyra St. Claire. Dan is with me. Please let us in."

The door opened a crack, and Lisa peered out at the street. "Did you bring the police?"

"No, but they'll be coming soon."

She sighed and pulled the door wider. Her face streaked with tears, shoulders hunched, and wearing sweats, Lisa no longer resembled the self-possessed orderly woman who worked at La Joliesse. She walked across the sparsely furnished room to a sofa that leaned to one side. "If you want a seat, you better use a kitchen chair," she mumbled.

"I won't drag this out. You took all my money and gave some of it to Symon. You're still in town, so you obviously knew you would be caught. Why did you need that much money?"

Lisa pulled an old cardigan tighter across her body and slumped onto a chair. "Symon is a gambler. He was in debt up to his eyeballs and desperate for money. He offered me a small share if I would give him the passwords to your bank accounts. I knew he was playing me for a patsy to take the fall, but I was desperate too. I put a small amount into his account so you could trace it, then took the rest for myself."

Lyra gazed around the room with its threadbare carpet and old appliances. "For you? I don't think so."

"You're so smart," Lisa said with a wishful smile. "I didn't want to cause you anymore misery, and I'm glad you got rid of that jerk Symon, but I desperately needed the money. My father is sick. He needs specialist care, and no matter how hard I work, there isn't enough money to pay for it. I'm sorry, but I already paid off all the outstanding debts and paid some in advance because I know I'll end up in jail. Maybe you could get that back."

The fact that she hadn't skipped town and intended to face up to her crime by not hiding, mollified Lyra. After all, what would she do to protect her mom? "I wish you'd come to me. I would have helped you."

The woman hung her head, and fat teardrops rained down on her lap. "I knew in my heart that you would but Duane wouldn't leave me alone. I was scared of him."

Lyra sat beside her and took her hand. "Do you know if Duane was in this with Symon?"

Lisa looked up and frowned. "What do you mean? Duane was the heavy, threatening to hurt me and my father."

"Was it Duane who told you about Symon needing money, or did Symon come and see you himself?" Lyra pressed. The pieces were finally starting to form the big picture. It was a slightly different scenario, but now it made more sense.

"It was always Duane who contacted me. I don't care about myself, but I couldn't bear the thought of my father being hurt anymore."

"So, none of this money went to Duane?"

"I figured Symon could pay him out of his amount. Him and that other goon who always has his face covered with a scarf."

"A tall slim man?"

"That's right."

"You came back to work the night of Suki's wedding. Was that man at La Joliesse at the time Kaden was run over?"

Lisa nodded. "He was in the alley yelling at Symon, who was so drunk he could barely stand."

Sirens sounded in the street, and Lyra stood.

"Thank you, Lisa, for being so honest. I'll get you a good lawyer, and please don't worry about the money or your father."

Her mouth opened and closed, and then Lisa burst into tears again. Lyra handed her a tissue and left her to the police who stormed through the door.

"Take it easy," Dan called as they handcuffed her. "The woman's been through enough."

Lyra smiled at him and then at Officer Denton. "Sorry to miss our appointment. Will now be a good time? I think we have all the information you need. Shall we meet at the station?"

He nodded, looking confused, then read Lisa her rights.

As they drove to the station, Lyra filled Maggie in on what had happened.

"I'm so glad you have your answers, and that Lisa isn't the horrible person I was imagining," Maggie said with a heavy sigh.

"Me too. It's a good feeling to have all the suspects out in the open and get a good look at their motives."

"Do you think you'll be in trouble with the police for taking matters into your own hands?"

"Maybe, but at this stage, I think they'll be more relieved that they can tie up all the loose ends. It turns out Symon's biggest problem was his gambling."

"Maybe not his biggest." Maggie snorted.

"Yes, he does have a few other faults," Lyra agreed.

"Ahh, what about the hit-and-run?" Dan reminded her.

"If Symon couldn't walk, he surely couldn't drive," Lyra reasoned.

"But I saw him," Dan protested.

"You saw a man wearing Symon's coat, in his car, wearing a scarf."

Dan's eyes bulged. "It was the other guy? The one Lisa mentioned?"

"That's right. The one who's been following me all this time—when it wasn't Duane. I think I know who did the driving, then took Symon to his house and put him behind the wheel. I bet Symon has no clue about much of that night."

Maggie stared at her. "Sheesh, you are way too good at this."

"Not good enough. People died, and I'm not sure La Joiesse will ever be the same."

"What do you mean? You had nothing to do with those deaths and surely you can work out something with the banks."

"The main problem, is the money is probably irretrievable. Without other revenue streams, I'm in big trouble because my overheads are huge. I can pay the current bills from the separate account kept for travel and personal expenses, but after buying that apartment it will leave me broke." Her voice hitched and Maggie wrapped her in a hug.

"Oh, Lyra. Surely you can work something out."

Something would have to give if she didn't want to borrow money or be penniless in a month's time. Then there was the sadness over how her fame was sullied and that one person was still out there.

Even with Cinnamon resting her head on Lyra's stomach and looking at her with eyes filled with love, she felt drained.

## 30

In the weeks following, Cinnamon stayed close to Lyra. Hugs were the order of every day and often every hour. There were some big decisions to make, and while she didn't shy away from them, one was so hard it made her almost physically ill. More than anything else, Cinnamon's presence helped her deal with that.

The police called and let her know that Symon refused to plead guilty to any of the charges and denied any knowledge of the money, as Lyra had predicted. The arson charge was never laid on him, since it was proven that Symon wasn't in Portland when it happened. His alibi was Rosetta Larkin. The case of hit-and-run would go to court, and Lisa assured Lyra through her lawyer that she would testify that the slim man had been there and he'd fought with a drunken Symon, who was incapable of driving. That didn't exonerate Symon completely, as far as Lyra was concerned, but she believed the truth would come out.

It was crunch time, and aware of this, Maggie shifted in the seat opposite Lyra.

"I'll understand if you need to let me go."

Lyra steepled her fingers on the blotter of her office desk. "Losing you isn't in my plans unless you've had enough."

"No way! I'll do whatever it takes to keep my job—any job —working for you," Maggie asserted.

Lyra smiled, which was the first time in a while. It faded when she heard people coming toward the room. "Here we go, Mags."

Maggie moved out of her chair and stood at the back of the room to make way for George and James.

"Come in and take a seat." Lyra took a steadying breath. "Please let me finish before you say anything."

The men glanced at each other and back at her. They knew about the lack of funds, and worry haunted their features. She wasn't sure if she could fix that, but she had to try.

"I've never hidden anything from you two, so you should be the first to know that I'm selling La Joliesse. Before you feel sorry for me, I'm not destitute. Symon and Lisa cleaned out a good deal of my resources, mainly to do with the restaurant. I'd say 'fortunately,' but you know what this place means to me."

George groaned, and she put up a hand to forestall him.

"However, what means more are the friendships I've made, especially with the two of you. And your loyalty. I appreciate all of it and know that it will be as hard for you to leave as it is for me. You will be paid up until the day I close the doors, and if I can help you in any way, you just have to say the word. Please know that any venture I undertake after this, you will be first on my list of staff to hire, but I'll understand if you'd rather not take the risk." The words barely made it out before the lump in her throat got so big, she thought she would choke.

George looked away, his Adam's apple jumping up and down.

"Let's not close the doors," James said quietly.

Lyra gulped hard. "I wish I had a choice, but I have creditors up the wazoo, and I don't want to go into more debt or use the last of the funds I do have."

"You're afraid of more repercussions?" James asked bluntly.

"I guess that's part of it." She sighed. "I have to regroup, and I can't do that any other way."

"Wouldn't you like to know that La Joliesse was still here?"

It wasn't like James to be unkind, but Lyra struggled not to take offence. "It would be nice, but a new owner will likely change the name and the menu."

"I wouldn't."

She blinked. "Pardon?"

James shrugged. "Let me buy her as she is. We'll split the debt by you selling her for a lesser price. The suppliers know me, and they'll be reasonable about extending credit."

The suggestion swirled around her. Was it feasible? "I don't mean to be indelicate, but how can you afford this?"

"I have a fair bit saved, and I may have an investor in the works." He winked at George. "You've given La Joliesse the best start. I'd like to continue in a similar vein. With a few twists, naturally."

Lyra shook her head. "You're serious?"

He nodded. "One hundred percent. We didn't want to mention it until you'd made your decision, in case we had things wrong. Let us have her."

She gulped again. "James, I couldn't imagine anyone I'd rather see here in my place."

He bowed, but not before she saw his eyes fill with tears. George could only nod.

James coughed, and he wiped his eyes on his sleeve. "I'll

put things into motion, and just so you don't worry, the rest of the staff will be asked to stay on as well."

"Thank you, James." Lyra smiled. "That eases my heart as well as my mind. I know you'll make this place even more successful."

He stood and shook her hand. "We'll have time to say goodbye, but I want you to know that it has been a pleasure to work for and with you."

George trudged out behind him, still clearly incapable of speech.

Maggie dabbed her eyes. "Well, that went well."

"Better than I could imagine." Lyra found a tissue in her bag and blew her nose. "I guess you and I have to decide where to go from here."

Maggie shrugged. "In my opinion, LA's never been your home."

Lyra didn't deny it. She'd moved here because that was where her show was filmed and then moved her mom out to be closer—which was another issue she had to face. The truth was, once Symon got a hold of her schedule, she saw less of the only family she had. "There's a lot of country to choose from. Any suggestions that won't take me too far away from Mom?"

"Portland is where your heart is, right?"

"I suppose it is, but since I dragged her away from Fairview to move here, that might be a bitter pill for Mom to swallow. Plus, I just bought a new apartment," Lyra reminded her.

Maggie snorted. "Which you haven't moved into, even though it's been ready for a week. You're basically packed, so you can literally go anywhere."

The wheels were already turning in Lyra's mind. "I guess it would be cheaper to get a new restaurant up and running there, where I wouldn't be in competition with La Joliesse. Or I could do something completely different."

"Exactly, and I know your mom wants you to be happy. There are so many options, and you've got time to think this through."

"I'm more confused now," Lyra mused.

"Okay, but you're good at solving mysteries. Why not treat this the same way? What do you want to do? Own a restaurant or work in one? Be a talk show host or do appearances, or both? Judge contests or maybe run them?"

Lyra's mind threatened to explode. Could she really make a new life from her old one? After years of being told what to do, except for La Joliesse, a life she could choose completely was incredibly tempting. "What about you?"

"I told you, find me a job and I'll go anywhere." Maggie smiled. "If it turns out that you don't need me, I'll understand and be grateful for being a part of your life for so long. I want you to be happy too."

Tears welled again, and luckily Lyra had more tissues. "You have to come wherever I go until you're totally sick of me."

Maggie sniffed. "Couldn't happen."

"Look at us." Lyra laughed as more of the weight lifted from her shoulders. "After all we've been through, this could be the start of a new adventure, and we're blubbering messes. Nothing's decided, but I feel we should celebrate."

"Count me in. What do you have in mind?"

"Kaden's grand reopening is on Saturday. I said I'd go. How do you think he'd feel if I turned up with a suitcase or two?"

Maggie grinned. "Are you kidding? He'll be thrilled."

"Then I guess we have a lot to do. First, I need to go see Mom."

"Don't you let her talk you out of this," Maggie warned.

So many things rolled around her head, but when Dan arrived, Lyra had already made a couple important decisions, which Cinnamon responded favorably to when asked for her opinion.

On the drive to her mom's small apartment, with the beagle beside her, she told Dan the news. "It may be a lot to ask, but I want you to come too. I have a few things I want to look into once we get there, and I'd like you at my side along with Maggie."

He glanced at her in the mirror. "Sheesh, that's a relief. I thought you were firing me."

"I can't imagine not having you around, Dan. But you might not feel that way when you understand that I have no idea how this is going to look."

Dan laughed. "Who wants a predictable life?" He parked in front of the complex and opened her door.

"I'm not sure how long I'll be. Will you wait for me?"

"See, how many bosses ask their staff that? I've got a good book and a comfortable seat to relax in." He winked. "It's not the worst job in the world."

Lyra smiled. She'd never really gotten a handle on the whole boss thing—unless she was cooking. That was a whole different story.

Having purchased the private and secure ground-floor apartment for her mom when she moved to LA, it was now apparent that not buying her own place was a sign that Lyra never viewed this town as her forever home.

When Patricia St. Claire opened the door and smiled in delight, Lyra's chest ached.

"Darling, I wasn't expecting you."

"I know, Mom, but this is important."

"I'm happy to see you any time. Is everything all right?" She ushered Lyra into a light and spacious sitting room, making sure to give Cinnamon plenty of attention.

Lyra sat and, without preamble, launched into the tough conversation. "I'm sorry not to give you more warning, but I'm leaving LA and moving back to Portland."

"What on earth for?" Her mom clasped a hand to her chest. "You're a star, and they all live here."

Having fallen in love with her daughter's celebrity status, it was naturally a shock that Lyra might consider giving it up. "Not all of them. Anyway, I've decided I don't want to be a star." She held up a hand when her mom started to interrupt. "Now, before you get too upset, I'll still write my recipe books and might even appear on a few shows if they ask. As long as I don't have to fly."

Patricia St. Claire did not see the humor. "Since I moved here to be close to you, this is a bit hard to take in."

"I know, but things have changed. The truth is I don't feel safe here anymore." Lyra didn't explain about La Joliesse. It was too painful to go over again, and she didn't want it to be common knowledge just yet. "After what happened to Kaden that night and the break-in at my apartment, can you blame me?"

Mom's eyes widened. "I'm sorry it's affected you so badly, and it was a horrible ending to such a beautiful day, but surely now that Symon is in custody, everything can go back to normal? Plus, you could hire more security."

Lyra shook her head. "I've thought of nothing else and can't see it getting better while I'm still around the same places, and I don't want to live that way."

They sat in silence for a few seconds. "It sounds like your mind is made up. Is this more to do with Kaden? After seeing the pictures of the two of you together, I wouldn't be surprised."

"Kaden is my best friend and that's it, Mom." Lyra sighed. "I've explained what Symon did and how he treated me. I need to feel in control again, and I think I'll have that away from here. Nothing will change for you, and I promise to come visit."

Patricia looked out the window to the tiny patch of lawn and gulped. "You don't like to fly, so things will change. Then again, I guess I don't see you that much, but I will miss knowing you're nearby if I need you."

Lyra's heart ached again. They'd been so close before she'd become famous, and she missed that. "You can visit me anytime. Won't it be nice to have a place to vacation?"

Her mom's face lit up. "Can Archie come?"

"Sure." She stood and leaned down to hug her mom. "Sorry to drop this on you and run, but I've got a lot to organize. I just wanted you to know, and I promise that as soon as I get a roof over my head, you can come stay for as long as you like."

"I'll be waiting" was the sad reply.

Lyra kissed her soft cheek. "Please don't tell anyone about my plans just yet, okay?"

"As if I would."

Lyra smiled, refraining from mentioning that she'd done that very thing before. More than once.

# 31

The flight to Portland was less traumatic because Lyra had so much to think about. Ironically, the plan to make her life simpler involved a lot of hard work. And plenty of anguish. Leaving La Joliesse wasn't quite as easy as she made out. Yet she couldn't deny that the excitement of a new adventure lifted her spirits. Her restaurant was in good hands.

Saying goodbye to people she loved and had a deep connection to made her heart ache. This was compounded by another visit to her mom, which went slightly better. They talked about places to live, and naturally Fairview cropped up. Lyra promised when her mom visited, she would take her there to catch up with the friends she hadn't seen in so long. It felt wrong to leave her behind, but it didn't have to be forever. Having made the decision to pull up stakes, she would see how it unfolded before she decided if she'd made a mistake.

Cinnamon snuggled into her side as they landed, and Lyra put her paperwork away.

"I hope you're looking forward to our new adventure as much as I am," she whispered.

Jim was already at the door by the time they were ready to disembark. Maggie shook his hand, but Lyra hugged him.

"I can't thank you enough for everything you've done. I'll miss you and Penny."

He smiled gently and gave Cinnamon a scratch between her twitching ears. "Who knows, I might lease the plane out to someone coming to Portland, and we can meet up for coffee. Of course, I'd have to smuggle Penny in the hold. Otherwise, she'd kill me."

"I'm sure she'd love that." Lyra laughed. "Seriously, you, Penny, and the kids must come visit me as soon as I'm settled."

He grinned. "You won't have to twist our arms. And heads-up, Penny will remind me plenty."

At the bottom of the steps, Dan accepted the keys for a hired car from the driver. The large, understated sedan was perfect and would fit the baggage they'd brought. Dan had arranged for all their furniture to go into storage until they had a place to deliver it, so all they had were a couple of suitcases each and Dan's duffel bag.

As far as she knew, no one had any knowledge that she was coming to town today. Even Kaden wasn't expecting her until tomorrow, so Phoenix was their first stop.

Colin grinned as soon as he saw her and led her through the restaurant. "He's in his office."

Like the last time, so many months ago, the kitchen went quiet when she walked in. There weren't as many staff today, as they were still getting set up, but they recognized her. She waved, then put a finger to her lips.

Oblivious to her arrival, Kaden was at his desk, bent over the menu.

"Glad to see Phoenix has finally risen from the ashes."

He bolted upright and stared for a heartbeat or two. "You're here already!"

"No need to check the date or worry I'll mess up your plans. I'm a day early, and I have a lot to do." Her rueful smile was enough to make him suspicious.

"Such as?"

She fussed with the clasp on her handbag. "Looking for a place to stay."

"You didn't book into your usual hotel?"

"I did, but I need something more permanent."

He blinked several times. "I don't understand."

"I'm coming home."

This time the silence dragged out while he grasped what she was saying. "But your restaurant…."

Her heart pinched, which she appreciated might happen for some time to come, but she smiled. "George and James have it under control. It turns out I'd rather be here."

With a whoop, he jumped from his chair. "I feel like I just won the lottery."

"Thank goodness I didn't walk away from my restaurant for nothing," she teased.

"I can't believe you did. Is it really permanent?"

"There is more to it, and I want to explain, but not now. How about you give me a tour of the new Phoenix? I won't stay long, and I'd offer to give you a hand today, but Maggie has some apartments for us to look at."

She could see he wanted more information, but she refused to put a damper on Kaden's reopening, and he let it go for now.

"There's no need. She's almost ready for business. We're merely adding the finishing touches." He showed her the modifications based on several things she'd done with La Joliesse that he'd admired.

"I love the changes. She's a thing of beauty. Not that she wasn't before the fire," Lyra added hastily.

"It's okay, I know what you mean. What I've done simply enhanced what was." He kept staring at her. "I can't believe you're really here."

"Believe it. I'll probably annoy you after a while, but can I come work tomorrow night for the reopening?" Lyra had a desperate need to be in a real kitchen like this one.

He gave a small bow. "I'd like nothing better, and you could never annoy me."

She laughed. "In that case, I'll see you tomorrow."

"Not tonight?"

"Sorry, I have a list a mile long. Moving is a bit more involved than I remembered, and I'd like to get a place relatively quickly."

"If you change your mind, you know where to find me. And I do want the lowdown on why this is happening."

"I promise. Just give me a little time to get my head around things."

He nodded, and she left Phoenix lighter of heart. This was only the second time in her life that she had leaped into something. The first was being talked into moving to LA, and the jury was still out on whether that had been as wise as she thought. Still, if she hadn't accepted the cooking show, she never would have had so many amazing opportunities.

Lyra truly didn't regret most of them, and the what-ifs wouldn't fix any of the bad things.

## 32

Maggie did well with the apartment hunting, as the first place she took Lyra to was perfect. It had a doorman and was over two floors with a patio area. Cinnamon raced around, barking her approval.

Lyra scratched the beagle's head. "I second that, Cin."

"It is pretty great," Maggie agreed.

"If we get it, you could stay in one of the extra bedrooms until we find you something suitable." Lyra looked at the price again. It would use most of her resources, which wasn't ideal.

Maggie followed her glance. "Why don't you think on it? We have more to view tomorrow, and since this one's been on the market a while, I don't think it will be snapped up in the next day or two."

The tightness in Lyra's shoulders lessened. "You're right. There's no urgency, and who knows what we might see tomorrow?"

"Exactly." Maggie shifted in her seat, then ran her hand along Cinnamon's back. "I should have mentioned this before, I wasn't feeling comfortable about staying in our usual places even with Symon locked up."

"I know what you mean," Lyra admitted. "We both know Symon couldn't be responsible for everything that happened because he couldn't be in two places at once."

"That's why I spoke to the manager and asked for more security. He was happy to oblige, but there will be an added cost."

"That's fine and I think it's worth the peace of mind." Lyra hoped this came out positively, but after they'd arrived at her suite she shivered.

"Do you want to go somewhere else?" Dan asked.

As much as she wanted to say yes, she had a reason for being here today, and she refused to back out of her plan no matter how scared she was that it might backfire. "It's natural to be on edge, but I'll be fine."

Despite her bravado, she followed Dan inside and waited thankfully while he checked out each room.

"I could stay the night in your suite if that would make you feel better," Maggie offered.

"You're just down the hall and so is Dan, but come by later and we'll have dinner together. I'll cook."

Once they'd gone, Lyra pulled out an empty folder and her laptop, which was the same brand as her last one. She fired it up and opened the file titled *New Life*.

Inside were all the things she had thought of as important criteria. It had started as a wish list, only now she decided it could be so much more. Traveling less was top of the list, followed by cooking more often. The idea of making dinner for Dan and Maggie already filled her with pleasure.

In fact, she decided to get a head start and whip up a batch of chocolate cupcakes, which were Maggie's favorite. The manager at each hotel she stayed at where there was a kitchen made sure to supply all the ingredients necessary for several dishes. She paid extra, but it was worth it.

Often, she had to bake to relieve the stress of travel or a show that had been taxing, and if she didn't get around to it, the ingredients were given to a local charity. Glad that she hadn't canceled that already, Lyra made a note to do so in the future. There were plenty of other corners she could cut as well.

While the cupcakes cooled, she added more suggestions to her list.

Teach others to bake with passion.

Get to know her mom again.

Spend as much time with Kaden as possible.

Find work for her friends that would make them as happy as she was going to be.

She plugged in the small portable printer and placed the printed pages in the folder. As much as she loved her laptop, she liked certain things in hard copy.

Next, she frosted the cupcakes and placed a cover over them, yawning the whole time. Since she hadn't been sleeping too well, Lyra decided a half-hour nap would perk her up enough to enjoy having dinner with her friends and discuss the move and everything that entailed.

Then she would face the night alone and see if her bait was taken.

Cinnamon's growl in her ear woke Lyra instantly. They were curled up on the bed, and long shadows lay across the room. Slowly, Lyra swung her feet to the floor, her hand remaining on Cinnamon's head to keep her quiet. Someone was in the sitting room, and Cinnamon wanted to get to them. Lyra put a finger on the beagle's muzzle, and the dog instantly quieted.

Lyra crossed the room, carpet muffling her steps. In the gloom of early evening, a figure held a folder and focused a penlight on it. Just as she suspected, here was the one person who had the ability to get near both Justine Long and Adam Lancaster without raising suspicions. She hadn't expected him until later tonight, which meant she really was on her own. Too late, Lyra appreciated that she should have at least told Dan her plans.

"Can I help you with something?" she said, simultaneously flicking the light switch.

Cameron Willett gasped, and the papers fell to the floor. "The d-door was unlocked."

Cinnamon growled loudly and stalked the intruder, backing him up to the table.

"That's not true. I checked it myself." Lyra's voice was firm, and his eyes narrowed.

"You weren't supposed to be here until tomorrow."

"Not many people knew that." She dangled the carrot, and he bit right away.

"Your mom did."

Lyra was disappointed but not surprised to have her fears confirmed. "So, you know Archie?"

Cameron shrugged. "Not well, but he's a helpful guy."

Lyra shook her head at his caginess. This was no time to get into a discussion about her mom's loyalty. "You set fire to Phoenix, didn't you?"

Cameron paled and sidestepped Cinnamon, but the beagle followed, her top lip curled back.

"What I don't understand is who you were trying to hurt. Kaden Hunter or me?" Lyra moved to the right until her hand was close enough to reach the lamp on the side table if it proved necessary.

"I don't care about him, but he shouldn't have gotten in the way. You helped him out instead of me."

"You're saying that you burned down his restaurant because I helped him with a wedding?"

"You worked in his restaurant all night and got all cozy with him for the photos."

"I hadn't seen him in a while, and we're good friends."

"The whole world saw what kind of friends you are!"

With a supreme effort, Lyra held back the anger threatening to burst out of her. She needed more time. "Whatever you believe is between Kaden and me would never be grounds enough to do the things you've done."

"You were supposed to have me on your show," he whined. "I was the runner-up, and you should have given me all the prizes when Adam died."

Suddenly she saw him as a petulant child. Always the helpful contestant and delighted for Adam when he'd won, he'd hidden this side of himself well.

"Adam was murdered, and there was no contingency at that time to cover it. Is that why you wanted to talk to me? To find out if that was a possibility so killing Adam would be worthwhile?"

He shrugged. "All I want is to be on your show and have a recipe book of my own."

"You could have done your book without me, and with all the trouble you've caused, the show's on hiatus. Indefinitely."

"If you hadn't met up with Kaden Hunter, that wouldn't have happened."

"Don't you dare say those murders were due to a chance meeting of a friend! Can't you hear how pathetic that is?"

He fisted his hands, and this time he ignored Cinnamon's growls. "I'm not the pathetic one, and I didn't intend to hurt either of them. Justine was a miserable wretch who was mean to everyone, including you. It wasn't acceptable. When

I saw how Adam treated you, I had to stop him. And now there's that pompous chef. How can you throw everything away for him? He's not half as good as you."

The rambling confession wasn't quite enough for Lyra. "Simplifying my life is why I'm moving. It has nothing to do with Kaden."

"Sure it does. First it was Symon who had you all tied up. Then you let that Adam fawn all over you, and now Kaden Hunter. Do you like to string men along? Is this all a game to you?"

His ugly condemnation of her character made the seriousness of her situation apparent, but she might not get another chance to get the whole truth. "You always played the nice guy, but you were the one wanting to win at all costs. Justine stood in your way, yet you could have legitimately beaten her in the contest."

He puffed out his chest. "I knew I could win, but I wanted her to leave you alone. I told her we should discuss our positions in the contest, and Justine agreed to meet with me in her room. She laughed in my face when I suggested she should be nicer. I pushed her and she tripped, so it really wasn't my fault."

It sounded too simplistic, but she let that go. "Okay, but why kill Adam when you did and not before he won?"

"Both of them dying before the winners were announced would have been too suspicious. As the runner-up, you can give me what I want—to work with you in your restaurant. It would be great publicity."

Lyra dropped the bomb with relish. "Except I've sold my restaurant."

"What? You sold La Joliesse? I don't believe you!"

His not knowing was what she'd been counting on. "It's the truth. When Lisa transferred all the money out of my account, selling was the only option."

He blinked rapidly and gulped. "I don't know what you're talking about. Your mom never said anything about that."

It was obvious he was lying, but she played along some more. "You mean to Archie? He's why I didn't tell her."

Cameron frowned. "How did you know he was telling me what was happening with you?"

"My friend Dan had him followed."

"If you knew about me, how come you didn't tell the police?"

"Actually, I wasn't sure until Lisa saw you with Symon. For the longest time, I thought he orchestrated everything. When I realized he couldn't have because with the tighter security, he didn't have access to Adam, I looked elsewhere. You are the common denominator."

"Why couldn't you accept that we would have made a good team? I could have been your co-host."

"Why would I want to work with an arsonist and a murderer?"

At his side, his fists opened and closed. "You made me those things. I was a good guy before then. I watched you for days, always looking over your shoulder. Then you let Adam win when it should have been me."

"There were other judges."

"Yeah, like they didn't listen to you."

Lyra licked her lips. Whatever he thought their connection was had now been severed. The glint in his eyes showed that Cameron disliked her intensely—probably even hated her. And without her restaurant, she was no use to him at all. Besides, he'd told her everything. There was no way he was going to walk away and leave her able to repeat it. Maybe she'd pushed a little too far, too soon.

"I'm sorry you feel the way you do, but it's time you left. I have friends coming by for dinner."

"That might be true, but I guess you're going to have to cancel."

Cameron came around the table like a big cat stalking its prey. The trickle of fear turned into a rushing river as blood pounded in her ears. Lyra hastily backed away, forgetting all about the lamp, until her heels touched the wall. She was trapped!

He reached out for her. In the blink of an eye, Cinnamon leaped from the sofa to his face, claws extended and raking. Cameron screamed and threw the beagle to the ground. Cinnamon whimpered, and Lyra dropped to her knees beside her, checking for broken bones.

"That savage beast has interfered for the last time." He ran to the kitchen and pulled a chef's knife from the block on the counter.

"Leave her alone!" Lyra yelled, searching for something to protect them and coming up with an overstuffed cushion. Not at all what she was hoping for, but she placed herself between them.

Cinnamon had other ideas. She jumped from the floor to the couch and onto the dining table, then flew through the air to land on the counter. The cover and cupcakes went flying, quite a few smashing over Cameron.

Then the apartment door burst open. Dan rushed in, followed by Maggie. Lyra had never been happier to see them. In seconds, Dan had the man on the floor, a knee in the middle of his back and Cameron's hands locked behind his head.

Maggie called the police while Lyra cradled Cinnamon.

"Are you all right, sweetheart?"

Cinnamon barked, which was the sweetest sound ever. Then again, the feisty beagle *was* covered in frosting. Her tongue proceeded to make short work of cleaning every morsel. Luckily she'd used an orange flavoured frosting.

The police arrived, and pandemonium erupted once more when they hauled the protesting criminal out in cuffs and a woman's scream came from somewhere down the hall.

Finally, after numerous questions and photos, the last policeman left.

Just as things calmed down, Kaden arrived. "Maggie messaged me. You're going to send me to an early grave if you keep putting yourself in danger."

"I didn't do it on purpose," she said in a muffled voice since her face was squashed in his shoulder.

He held her at arm's length. "Didn't you?"

Lyra flushed a little. "Okay, I had the idea that once I got back to Portland, Cameron would try to get in here. Other people were getting hurt, but I honestly believed it was ultimately me who was the target."

"How could you run the risk by doing this without backup—preferably the police?"

"I couldn't be sure he would take the bait, and Maggie and Dan were expected any minute. Besides, Cinnamon was here to back me up. She did an awesome job too. That's why she's in such a mess."

"Attacked by cupcakes." Maggie snorted. "Who would have thought of them as weapons?"

Dan joined her at the counter, where they found a couple undamaged ones and proceeded to eat them.

Kaden raised an eyebrow but still wasn't amused. "This was dangerous at best. And how did you know it was Cameron?"

"By the process of elimination. Obviously I didn't know for sure, but this was an opportunity to test my theory, because the only person other than Maggie, Dan, and Jim who knew I was coming here today was Mom. She promised not to say anything, but she would have mentioned it in confidence to the guy she's dating, and I know Archie leaked stuff before. Turns out I was right. I'm convinced that Cameron's been paying him for some time, which is how he always knew my whereabouts."

"Aren't you Ms. Sherlock?" Kaden frowned. "I wish you'd told me your plans. Didn't you trust me?"

"Don't be silly. You three are the ones I trust most, but I knew you'd try to talk me out of it. My biggest regret is that it took so long to get this far. Adam might still be alive if I'd figured out who killed Justine."

"No one could have known that he was out there stalking you all this time," Kaden growled. "There is something else. I'm not sure how much she's been involved in all this, but downstairs, I saw them taking Rita into custody."

Lyra's head was spinning. "What's she doing here?"

"She was wearing a maid's uniform, so I suspect she stole the manager's code and let Cameron in. Fortunately, after the last break-in, the hotel installed new security cameras, and the manager was talking to the sergeant, saying they showed Rita hanging around these rooms."

Lyra shook her head in disgust. "So that's how he got in here. I can't believe how many people were involved in bringing me down."

Kaden pulled her into his arms. "You bravely got to the bottom of things, and with them all behind bars, you'll finally be safe." He scratched Cinnamon between the ears. "Both of you."

Lyra laughed at her precious pooch, who wiggled in between them, smearing frosting along the way. To be fair, she had attempted to lick most of it off. "You're right, I'm lucky to have such good friends. And I'm also grateful that beagles love cupcake crimes."

Maggie snorted while the men grinned. Lyra hugged the beagle, determined to look forward to a new beginning where fame wasn't everything, and where friends and family knew they were always more important than money.

Thanks so much for reading Beagles Love Cupcake Crimes the first book in the Beagle Diner Mysteries series. I hope you enjoyed it!

If you did…

1 Help other people find this book by leaving a review.

2 Sign up for my new release e-mail, so you can find out about the next book as soon as it's available and receive the bonus epilogue! If you've previously joined, don't worry, you'll be able to get it very soon for free.

3 Come like my Facebook page.

4 Visit my website caphipps.com for all of my books.

5 Keep reading for an excerpt from Book 2 Beagles Love Steak Secrets.

# BEAGLES LOVE STEAK SECRETS

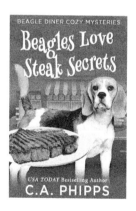

The Diner was full of the lunch time crowd. It had been this way ever since Lyra hung the open sign on her door a few months ago. It seemed that the small town of Fairview was still curious about the ex-celebrity chef. The first few weeks were more about the press than the food and she was glad when that died down.

Many of the locals found the opening exciting and came out in their Sunday best, hoping to be seen on the news or feature in a paper somewhere. Naturally, there were one or two who took umbrage at the town being turned upside down, but no one could argue that the hustle and bustle had been good for every business.

Maggie Parker sat outside the back of the diner at a table in the corner of the pet friendly covered veranda. She was working away on Lyra's latest cookbook and keeping an eye on the customers out there. Lyra's beagle, Cinnamon, sat at Maggie's feet and whenever anyone came by, she introduced herself. Seated in this prime position in the center of town since day one, the beagle was already well known.

Lyra dropped off an order and hurried back to the counter inside.

"Are these fresh?"

Lyra blinked in surprise. Arabelle Filmore was a cranky woman in her sixties, who'd adopted the ageist get out of jail free card by saying what she thought whenever she felt like it.

"The cupcakes are just out of the oven, Ms. Filmore."

Arabelle sniffed. "If that were true the frosting would be melting."

"Did you want one?" Lyra held a set of tongs in her hand, thinking what she'd like to do with them had nothing to do with food, but smiled instead.

"Don't rush me, I'm still thinking about it."

"Take as long as you need." Lyra put the tongs down. The problem with waiting for Arabelle was that she refused to move out of the way and the line grew.

"I'll get my usual, please," Robert McKenna called over the top of the tiny woman's head.

"You wait your turn, Robert Mckenna!" Arabelle scolded.

He shrugged. "If we did that every time you dithered around in here, we'd starve."

Arabelle looked him up and down and sniffed. "I can't see that happening."

Probably a similar age as Arabelle, Rob was as fit as a man half his age. Grinning he patted his slightly rounded stomach. "It's all bought and paid for, Belle. Thanks for noticing, though."

Arabelle sucked in a large breath. "Don't you dare call me that!"

Rob laughed. "You were Belle as a kid and, as far as I'm concerned, still Belle now."

Feathers well and truly ruffled, Arabelle's mouth opened and closed several times. Being lost for words was a sight Lyra hadn't seen before. She took that moment to send Rob's order through to the kitchen then waited, along with every customer in ear shot, for Arabelle to focus.

"All that fat will kill you," Arabelle finally managed through clenched teeth.

Rob took a seat and blew her a cheeky kiss. "You're such a caring woman, can't think why you haven't been snapped up long ago."

"That man has no respect," Arabelle grumbled. "I'll have my usual."

Lyra had to bite her lip yet wasn't surprised by the choice. No matter what caught her eye, Arabelle always had tea and a berry friand.

From where he sat, Rob rolled his eyes and Lyra had to look away as she took the money. The two of them were as funny as a play and if it didn't run every day, it would certainly be odd around here.

The waitress hurriedly cleaned the table that Arabelle preferred which had fortunately become vacant. Twenty-year-old, Poppy received no thanks and moved on to take orders from the diners who waited with a good deal more patience and politeness. Having a sweet but no-nonsense disposition, Poppy was perfect for the job of waitress and barista. It meant that Lyra was comfortable leaving her to deal with the diners so she could get back to the kitchen to ensure the orders weren't backing up.

This was the beauty of a small business. She could cook or chat with her customers or spend time on a new recipe when things were quiet. After a horrendous few months dealing with two different types of crimes, she concluded that her previous life as a celebrity chef and show host was overrated. She did miss her famous LA restaurant, La Joliesse, but she could cook anywhere and that's what meant the most to her—not fame, which went hand in hand with being hounded by fans and paparazzi. Just the thought made her shudder

Even with her daily dose of Arabelle, which Lyra tried not to inflict on her staff, she didn't regret her decision to move from LA to Fairview instead of staying in Portland, her original choice, and opening a more upmarket restaurant rather than a diner.

This pretty town lay halfway between there and Destiny to the south and meant a huge change of life for not only herself but some of her staff. Most remained at La Joliesse after the sale, while a couple opted to join her in this adventure. Of course, Fairview was Lyra's childhood home, so she did have an advantage over the others.

The main street had a cross intersection in the middle and a few more roads bisecting each arm of it. Several businesses were two-storied with apartments above them, but most were single-storied like the diner. At the back was the veranda Lyra added to make the covered dining area. Behind this was a gravel carpark and path, then a hedge and, slightly visible beyond, was an old farmhouse. This was Lyra's home, and it couldn't be more convenient.

The day she'd driven here on a whim, with her assistant, Maggie, and her driver, Dan, they found a run-down diner and derelict farmhouse. A conglomerate working with the town committee was buying up the businesses and Rob Mckenna persuaded Lyra to purchase the diner, thereby saving it and possibly the town. Dramatics aside, the local lawyer made it happen that day and once the bill of sale came through, the rest was history.

The farmhouse took a bit longer to buy since the owners had to be tracked down, but within a month it was hers. Still a work in progress the house had to wait because the diner needed a top to toe refit which had to come first.

Rolling out the pastry for her butter chicken pies, Lyra marveled, at the change in the diner from front to back now that it was finished.

A hand touched her shoulder. "You're miles away."

Lyra dropped the rolling pin on her foot and yelped.

Cinnamon barked from the doorway.

"Sorry, I didn't mean to startle you."

"I'm okay," she said to both of them. "I was thinking about all the changes and how I still can't believe how far we've come in such a short time."

Maggie grinned. "Shall I pinch you?"

"No need for more violence. Besides, I know by my rough hands that I'm working harder than I ever have."

"You don't seem upset by that. No regrets?"

"Not yet. How about you?"

Maggie grinned again. "How you talked me into this I'll never know, but I am glad about it."

Lyra smirked. "I don't remember twisting your arm."

"I admit it's way less stressful than making sure your itinerary didn't blow out and that you had everything you needed for each trip. Now I get to work on the book and the house which are both things I love."

"I'm glad too." Lyra cut the pastry to line the two dozen pans set out on the counter. "You're an amazing designer and doing this without you might have been a game changer."

"I doubt that" Maggie argued, while looking pleased. "You love a challenge."

"I guess that must be true since I've had plenty of them."

Maggie snorted. "There were definitely several that you could have done without but look how much you've achieved in a few months."

Lyra glanced around her and nodded. "I guess I have to accept that my previous life paid for all this and be grateful."

All she'd wanted was to live in peace doing what she loved and now that's exactly what she had. Of course, it couldn't be so successful without her staff. In the doorway, Poppy retied her hair then she washed her hands. The girl was a quick learner, could never do enough, was adored by Cinnamon and keen to learn to cook. Likewise, the dishwasher, Earl, who with his learning difficulty was simply happy to have a job and often cleared tables if they got swamped. Leroy, her cook, was the major find, thanks to Rob. Hiring him meant he could handle the grill which left her to concentrate on the baking.

As if fate decided there was too much happiness going on, the back door opened, and Dan burst in.

"There's been a flood in the house."

Maggie gasped and ran out the door behind him.

Lyra ripped off her apron. "Will you be okay, Leroy?"

"Get going, I'm under control here and the others will help."

Lyra didn't doubt her chef. Leroy was a blessing. He took it in his stride when she ducked in and out of the diner to take care of house queries and to work on her book. Finding him made running a diner instead of a restaurant more palatable than she had ever imagined.

After throwing a damp cloth over the pastry, she ran after Dan and Maggie.

Read Beagles Love Steak Secrets TODAY!

# RECIPES

These recipes are ones I use all the time and have come down the generations from my mum, grandmother, and some I have adapted from other recipes. Also, I now have my husband's grandmother's recipe book. Exciting! I'll be bringing some of them to life very soon.

Just a wee reminder, that I am a New Zealander. Occasionally I may have missed converting into ounces and pounds for my American readers.

My apologies for that, and please let me know—if you do try them—how they turn out.

Cheryl x

# CHOCOLATE CARAMEL CUPCAKES

## Ingredients

1 cup/130 g plain flour
½ cup/40 g cocoa
½ teaspoon baking powder
½ teaspoon baking soda
¼ teaspoon salt
½ cup/113 g melted butter (unsalted)
½ cup/100g white granulated sugar
½ cup/100g dark brown sugar, packed
2 large eggs, room temp
2 teaspoons vanilla extract
¾ cup / 180ml buttermilk
Salted Caramel Ingredients
2¼ cups/250g chewy caramels
½ cup thickened cream
1 teaspoon sea salt

## Instructions

1 Preheat your oven to 180C / 350F . Grease your muffin pans or insert paper cases.

2 In a bowl, sift together the flour, cocoa, baking soda, baking powder and salt. Mix well to combine.

3 In another bowl beat together the melted butter and both sugars until smooth. Add eggs one at a time, beating well after each one. Add the vanilla and beat to combine.

4 Add ⅓ of the flour mixture to the butter and sugar mixture. Stir through gently until just combined. Now add half of the buttermilk, mix gently. Continue adding some of each until all the flour and buttermilk is combined. Do not overmix.

5 Half fill the cupcake cases. Bake in the oven for around 18-20 minutes.

6 Cool in the tin for 5 minutes before turning out onto a cooling rack

### Ingredients for Buttercream and Salted Caramel

7oz /200 g softened unsalted butter
¼ cup/50 g brown sugar
½ cup salted caramel
2 ½ cups confectioners' sugar
1 teaspoon vanilla extract
2 tablespoons thickened cream
½ teaspoon plain salt

### Salted Caramel Instructions

• Place the unwrapped caramels and cream in a saucepan over low heat. Heat, stirring until the caramels melt and the mixture is smooth. Add the salt and stir through. Allow to cool before using.

### Buttercream Instructions

• Beat the butter and sugar together until lightened and fluffy (4-5 minutes). Make sure to scrape down the sides of the bowl as necessary.

• Add 1/2 cup of the (cooled) salted caramel and beat well to combine.

• With the mixer on low, add the icing sugar 1 tablespoon at a time until fully incorporated. Beat on medium-high for 2 minutes, scraping down the sides of the bowl from time to time.

• Finally, add the vanilla, cream and salt and beat to combine

**Assembling**

• Using a sharp knife, cut a hole in the top of each cupcake. Fill with approximately 1 teaspoon of salted caramel. Top the cake you removed.

• Pipe buttercream on the top and drizzle with salted caramel.

# OTHER BOOKS BY C. A. PHIPPS

**The Maple Lane Cozy Mysteries**

Sugar and Sliced - Maple Lane Prequel

Apple Pie and Arsenic

Bagels and Blackmail

Cookies and Chaos

Doughnuts and Disaster

Eclairs and Extortion

Fudge and Frenemies

Gingerbread and Gunshots

Honey Cake and Homicide - preorder now!

**Midlife Potions - Paranormal Cozy Mysteries**

Witchy Awakening

Witchy Hot Spells

Witchy Flash Back

Witchy Bad Blood - preorder now!

**Beagle Diner Cozy Mysteries**

Beagles Love Cupcake Crimes

Beagles Love Steak Secrets

Beagles Love Muffin But Murder

Beagles Love Layer Cake Lies

**The Cozy Café Mysteries**

Sweet Saboteur

Candy Corruption

Mocha Mayhem

Berry Betrayal

Deadly Desserts

Please note: Most are also available in paperback and some in audio.

# ABOUT THE AUTHOR

*'Life is a mystery. Let's follow the clues together.'*

C. A. Phipps is a USA Today best-selling author from beautiful New Zealand. Cheryl is an empty-nester living in a quiet suburb with her wonderful husband, 'himself'. With an extended family to keep her busy when she's not writing, there is just enough space for a crazy mixed breed dog who stole her heart! She enjoys family times, baking, and her quest for the perfect latte.

Check out her website http://caphipps.com

**f** X ⊙

Made in the USA
Monee, IL
11 August 2024